NO RETURN

NO RETURN

No Justice Series: Book 4

NOLON KING
DAVID WRIGHT

STERLING & STONE

To YOU, the reader.
Thank you for your support.
Thank you for the wonderful emails.
Thank you for the thoughtful reviews.
Thank you for reading and loving our stories.

Wednesday August 28

Prologue

JESSI PRICE STARED out the window of her mom's SUV wishing she could sit at the bus stop like a normal kid.

Destinee laughed and pointed at Rodney, one of the funniest kids they knew. He was chasing Amber Carrington with something on the end of a stick.

"Oh, my God. I think it's dog poop!" Destinee looked at Jessi.

The thought of the snobby, awful, Amber Carrington getting poop on her overpriced clothes made Jessi laugh.

"He got some on her!" Destinee squealed.

Jessi watched her best friend and felt bad she was stuck in the SUV. Destinee would rather be leaning on the guard rail in front of the pond with the other kids, be *in* on the fun instead of watching from afar.

She made eyes with her mom in the rearview. "Come on, Mom, can't we just sit there for a few minutes."

"Be glad I'm even letting you ride the bus. Eventually, things can go back to normal. Just … not yet."

Not yet.

A familiar phrase ever since Paul Dodd destroyed Jessi's

life and killed her father last year. She'd survived her abduction, yet it seemed that life would never be normal again. Any time Jessi asked to do anything, or go anywhere, the answer was always the same.

Not yet.

"It's okay," Destinee said, "I don't mind sitting in here. Plus, it's air conditioned."

Not that it was hot.

"Thank you," her mom said.

Jessi looked down at her backpack, wanting to pull out her stuffed pink unicorn and hug it. HappyCorn was Jessi's secret. Even Destinee didn't know about the stuffie her father had given her a few years ago that she now smuggled to school in her backpack. Knowing that HappyCorn was in there gave Jessie the strength to return. But she was ten and felt silly admitting it to anyone.

As Destinee kept watching the other kids goofing around, Jessi's eyes focused on her blue-and-yellow striped tights, tracing a finger over a slight change of color where two of the lines met to see if the material was raised there or if it was an optical illusion.

Just an illusion.

Destinee laughed louder and harder, stoking Jessi's anger.

"Please, Mom? You can stay right here. You can watch us the whole time."

"Sorry."

"Come on, nobody's going to take us. Nobody is going to do anything with that cop sitting *right there.*"

Jessi looked back at the unmarked patrol car. Today it was blue. She couldn't really see the officer behind the wheel, but she didn't need to — it was one of the people looking out for her.

"I don't want to talk about it anymore." Her mom sighed and stared out the window.

"He's in jail," Jessi said. "He's not coming back."

"No more." Her reflection glared from the rearview. "Be glad I'm letting you take the bus."

"It's okay," Destinee said again.

She was nine, one year younger than Jessi, but in the same grade and taller. Most people thought she was at least eleven. Jessi wasn't sure if people pegged Destinee as older because she was a tomboy and played a lot of sports or if it was because she was a big sister to her four-year-old brother.

Sometimes, she acted like *Jessi's* big sister, like when she agreed with her mom and said stuff like, "it's okay" or "your mother is only looking out for you."

Times like that, Jessi wanted to tell her to mind her own business, that she wasn't her older sister. And that's when she was tempted to remind Destinee of her age.

But Jessi never complained, because Destinee was one of the few kids who didn't tease her or ask a lot of questions about what happened with that man.

Being with Destinee was what it was like *before* him. They hung out, made each other laugh, and talked about normal kid stuff, not horrors that Jessi only half remembered, usually when waking from nightmares. Horrors she was trying to put behind her. But it was hard to move on when people no longer saw you as you, but rather, *that girl* — someone to be pitied, whispered about, and sometimes, for reasons Jessi might never understand, *teased*.

Jessi spotted the bus rolling down the block. She unbuttoned her seatbelt, grabbed her backpack, and leaned between the front and back seats to give her mother a kiss. "Bye. Love you, Mom."

Seconds later, she was following Destinee out her door.

"Have a good day, girls."

Destinee turned to wave. "Goodbye, Mrs. Price!"

Jessi closed the door and followed Destinee toward the other kids, lining up for the bus.

As they approached, she could feel the eyes on her and Destinee, but mostly her. At least they weren't whispering so much these days. That was the worst, because as much as Jessi wanted to ignore the comments and speculations, a part of her *wanted* to engage them, to know what they were saying.

But Mom ordered her to ignore them.

The bus squealed to a stop.

The door opened and Francine, a heavyset black woman in her late fifties, greeted each group of kids with "Good morning." Most of the kids echoed the sentiment, but only barely. Jessi always smiled when she saw Francine, remembering the time she intervened when kids were overwhelming her after she first returned to school, on a day when Destinee wasn't there to protect her.

"Good morning, Francine," Jessi said as she climbed aboard.

She and Destinee found a seat in the middle of the bus, their usual spot, with Jessi taking the window seat. As Amber boarded with her bestie, Kayla, the girls stared at Jessi, trading whispers and giggles.

Destinee glared up at them. "Got something to say?"

Amber must have smelled something rotten, the way her nose tried to crawl back into her face. She shook her head, rolled her eyes, and said, "Whatever."

Then the girls passed.

Destinee watched them, balling her fist. "You sure you don't want me to hit her? I will."

"It's not worth it," Jessi said.

She secretly liked that Destinee was willing to defend

her but didn't want her friend getting into trouble. Not just for Destinee's sake — her parents were cool — but for Jessi's. If being outside the house became an issue, then back to homeschooling it was.

And Jessi *hated* homeschooling.

Being home all day and all night reminded her of everything she went through. All that she'd lost.

Rodney was sitting with his friend, Jack, one seat in front of them. He turned around. "'Sup? Did you see what I did to Amber?"

Destinee laughed. "That was *sooooo* awesome. Did you get any on her?"

"No. I just wanted to scare her."

Jessi was sure Destinee liked Rodney, even though she said "eww" whenever it was suggested.

They talked about the latest *Star Wars* movie, which Jessi hadn't seen. That one or any of them. But she liked listening to the conversations, even they didn't always make sense.

A white van with blacked-out windows kept pace beside the bus. Jessi tried to ignore it, but it was going so much slower than all the other cars. And maybe whoever was on the other side of those tinted windows was watching them.

Rodney caught her stare. "Whachya lookin' at?"

"That van. It's driving so slow. Can you see inside?"

Now all four of them were looking.

"No," Destinee said. "But there's nobody in front of them."

"Probably a pedo van." Jack laughed.

Jessi had never heard that term, nor did she know where Rodney got it from, but she could put two and two together. Still, that wasn't her first thought. Not when someone could drive by, look up, and see *that girl* — Jessi

Price. The one from the news. The one who had those terrible things happen to her.

Jessi got that look a lot when she went out. Sometimes people, actual adults, would come up and say something, like "I'm so sorry" or "You're such a brave girl."

Sometimes she even saw people sneak photos of her with their phones, like they were going to tell their friends, "Hey, look who I saw."

She suffered the worst sort of celebrity.

Rodney and Jack both offered the driver their fingers.

Destinee laughed and added a third.

Some other kids saw what they were doing and joined the salute.

Jessi's shoulders tightened, her stomach filling with butterflies.

She wanted to plead with them to stop, to avoid angering the driver.

Maybe he was an old man who would look up and see them all flipping him the bird. Maybe he'd follow the bus to the school and report them, and they'd *all* get in trouble.

The van lurched forward and sped away.

The boys laughed.

Her shoulders relaxed.

The bus kept rolling as her friends talked about their PE teacher, each taking turns imitating the way he was always yelling at the kids.

Jessi could finally exhale and surprised herself with a laugh. Their impressions, especially Jack's, was spot on.

A few blocks later, as the road narrowed from four lanes to just two, the bus stopped a full block short of a stop sign.

And it wasn't moving.

Jessi looked up, past the bus driver.

A white van was stopped in the road, parked sideways,

occupying both lanes. Smoke poured from the engine, the driver standing in front of its raised hood, shaking his head.

Was it the same white van? Its windows were blacked out, just like the other one.

Her heart was racing.

Her shoulders tightened again.

A cold chill rippled through her core.

Destinee looked at Jessi. "You okay?"

"Something's wrong."

"What?" She followed Jessi's gaze. "The van?"

The driver had his back to them, covered in a blue hoodie. Then he turned and started walking toward the bus. Francine looked over at him as he approached her door.

Don't open it. Don't open it. Don't—

She didn't need to.

He forced the door open.

Francine started to stand. "What are you—"

She never finished her question.

The man's hand emerged from his jacket, and before Jessi could register what he was holding, the muffled gunshot made a hollow pop and sent Francine falling back, her blood painting the window behind her.

Children screamed.

Jessi sat frozen, mute and staring ahead.

Chaos. Kids in the front running toward the back, as the man raised his gun.

He was wearing a blue ski mask under the hoodie. And she could only see his scary brown eyes.

He fired another shot into Francine's body, then yelled, "Quiet, or I start shooting you!"

Silence.

Except for the whimpering.

Jessi was still quiet.

Terrified, and unable to move, breathe, or swallow.

Movement to her left, then Destinee pulled her arm from Jessi's grasp. "Ow!"

Jessi hadn't realized she'd been clutching Destinee's arm, let alone clawing at her skin.

"All right," said their attacker, "this'll be over fast. One thing, then I'm outta your hair."

The kids stared in silence.

Jessi's mind was a mess, flashing back to when that man had stolen her. She saw flashes of things she'd thought she'd forgotten — Paul touching her in places he shouldn't. Then ready to do it again in front of the detective, Mallory Black.

And then there were his eyes.

Were they blue? Or brown?

She could only remember the ice inside them, and a terrifying hunger she could not understand.

"I'm looking for someone on this bus. Maybe you all can help me."

A warm puddle beneath her.

The bus was quiet enough for Jessi to hear her heart pounding.

She wondered if everyone else could hear it. Or smell the pee.

How long until Destinee felt it seeping over to her side.

Still, Jessi couldn't move. Could barely breathe. She couldn't move her eyes from the man with the gun.

"I'm looking for Jessi Price. Is she on this bus?"

Every kid turned and looked right at her.

Her heart froze.

The man started down the aisle, his gun on Jessie.

She shook her head and stuttered, "No, no, no, no."

This couldn't be happening.

Was it Paul Dodd? Had he come back to finish what he'd started?

She tried to tell if the man's eyes were the same color as the monster's.

Why can't I remember?

He was four rows away, and every bit of her was screaming to stand up and run.

But her body refused to listen. Or do anything at all.

Someone stop him.

Someone do something!

But nobody else moved, either.

And then he was there, staring down at Jessi, gun aimed at her head.

This is it.

He's going to kill me.

She wanted to ask why, wanted to beg for her life. But her mouth would only make the word *No*, over and over.

Destinee stood up beside her. "Leave her alone!"

She took a swing at the man.

He raised the gun and—

No!

—fired.

Destinee fell back against the window, her eyes wide in disbelief.

Destinee!

Jessi stared, mute, a pain in her throat strong enough to split her in two.

She reached out to help her friend, to do something, but he grabbed her by the hair and yanked Jessi out of the seat.

Rodney reached for his gun.

The man hit him hard in the head and shoved the weapon in his face. "Anyone else wanna be a dead hero?"

The world was frozen.

11

Jessi couldn't take her eyes off of Destinee's glassy stare. She looked down at her hands, covering her stomach, blood soaking her shirt.

The man dragged Jessi backwards. "Let's go."

She wanted to scream, but who could help her as the man carried her off the bus?

He threw her in the back of his van and slammed the doors.

It was dark inside, and she blindly searched for a handle.

Then movement behind her.

Someone else is in the van!

Hands pulled her back.

She struggled, squirming, kicking out, finally able to scream, incoherent as it was.

A gunshot outside the van …

Are the police here to save me?

Did they hear me?

… preceded another three.

Then a hand was covering her mouth, and in it, something cold and wet, smelling like strong chemicals. Maybe gas.

A sweet scent coated her throat as she struggled to break free.

And then her fight was all gone.

The last thing Jessi felt was the van bouncing over something on the ground as it peeled into traffic.

Prologue 2

JASPER WOKE ALONE in a dark room, hands tied behind him, sitting in a chair with a bright light burning into his eyes.

Everything was fuzzy — his vision and how he'd gotten here.

Loud electronic music thrummed from somewhere nearby, tickling his bare feet.

Every part of his body throbbed. He'd been battered, cut, and water boarded to within an inch of his life, a release from the pain only seconds away if only he would "just fucking tell them."

What these men wanted him to say, Jasper wasn't sure. It was all so vague.

Suddenly, he realized he wasn't alone.

Metal scraped against the concrete floor.

Jasper looked to the right and saw his punisher. A tall, bald man with a Hispanic accent and a black tattoo under his eye, some symbol he did not recognize.

He dragged his machete against the concrete. "You ready to tell us?"

"Fuck you."

The man came at Jasper, swinging the machete, slicing through his neck.

Hot blood jetted out of his arteries. Jasper went into shock.

No!

The man swung again, and again, until Jasper was no longer conscious. The last thing he sensed was his head leaving his body and falling onto the concrete.

Then he woke with a scream.

It was the second time in a week Jasper had the dream. But this was a vision, and that meant it would happen. He could feel it with the same certainty that had filled his marrow every time before.

But he didn't know who the man was, what he wanted to know, or when it would happen.

And thus Jasper couldn't prepare for it or do anything to protect himself.

Friday, August 23

Chapter 1 - Mallory Black

Five days ago...

"Why are you calling me?" Mal asked. "Is this some sort of game?"

"No," Jasper answered. "I'm calling because you need me."

"Why do I need you?"

"So you can stop Dodd before it's too late."

"What are you talking about? He's in jail, awaiting trial."

"Something bad is going to happen."

"What?" This was really pissing her off.

"He's going to kill her."

"*Who?*"

"Jessi Price."

"He's in jail."

"He won't be for long. And when he gets her, he'll finish what he started. He wants you to watch him hurt then kill her. And then he's going to do the same to you."

Mal wanted to yell at Jasper, accuse him of being a crackpot. He was obviously obsessed with her, Dodd, and the case. Maybe it had to do with ghosts of his former career. She knew plenty of ex-cops haunted by cases they never solved. Maybe this was exacerbated by his daughter's suicide and the feelings of powerlessness it surely gave him.

Regardless of his root obsession, it was absurd to believe Dodd could get out of prison, let alone grab Jessi again. And then somehow Mal, too.

But she wasn't about to argue.

Not when she could placate him, maybe get him to come in. Then she could arrest him for the murder of Wes Richardson and figure out if he had anything to do with the disappearance of Calum Kozack and his girlfriend, Brianna — the parties rumored to be responsible for driving Jasper's daughter to suicide.

"Okay. Why don't you come in and we can talk about it?"

Quiet on the other line. Then a laugh. "Come on, detective. You know I was a cop, right?"

"So, what do you want from me?"

"Two options, way I see it. Kill him before he can get out. Before any of this happens. Or … you get someone to kill him."

"Is that where your offer of 'help' comes in? You planning a trip?"

Another laugh, this one weary. "No. I already know you won't do either of those things. I'm just warning you not to stop me the next time our paths cross. I will take him out."

Mal couldn't imagine the sequence of events that could possibly put her in such a situation again — restrained to a bed as Dodd was about to rape that poor child.

Or Jasper coming in to save the day, offering her another chance to slay the dragon.

"Um, okay, sure. Why don't we meet somewhere? We can talk about what you think might happen."

"You still don't believe me. But you will. In the meantime, maybe get some protection on Jessi. As much as you can."

"I need more details. When is he getting out? How? Or taking Jessi?"

"I … I don't know the details, exactly. She only told me bits and pieces."

"She being your daughter?"

"Yes," he said.

"So, what's the deal? Is she a psychic or something?"

Not that Mal believed it, but *he* certainly seemed to.

"I don't want anything happening to her. So let's not talk about her."

"I just need to know what I'm working with here."

"You know I know *something*, right? I reached out before any of this even started, *before* he took your daughter. I tried to warn you. And then I showed up when he took you."

"Maybe you're working with him. Maybe you're in some secret sex club."

A beat, then a sigh. "I'm sure you've looked into me enough to know that's not the case."

"Well, I dunno, Mr. Parish, my intel says you died in a fire. And yet, here we are. You'll forgive me if I'm not entirely certain what to trust."

"I haven't lied to you yet. And I haven't been wrong."

"You or your daughter?"

"*We* haven't been wrong."

"I need more information. Something I can work with. You don't know how or when Dodd will get out of jail. You don't know how or when he'll take Jessi. What am I

supposed to do? Tell my bosses this psychic I know says we need to watch out? Without specifics, no one is going to listen."

"As I said, A or B."

"You expect me to kill him?"

"Or have someone do it for you. Surely you know *someone* who could get the job done."

"I'm a cop. I don't go around calling hits. Forgive me for asking, but were *you* really an officer of the law?"

"He *needs* to die."

"Like Wes?"

Silence for a moment, then, "Are we going over that again?"

"Okay, let's skip that one for now. How about a couple of missing young adults? Names are Calum Kozack and Brianna Gilchrest. They just so happened to have both known your daughter. Did *they* need to die?"

Silence.

And then he was gone.

Chapter 2 - Mallory Black

MAL COULDN'T GO BACK to sleep after Jasper's call.

He was bat-shit for sure, but somehow the man knew things he shouldn't.

She went to work early and put in a few calls, first to check up on Dodd in the jail and make sure he was still behind bars. Then to Jessi's mother, to make sure everything was fine there. Colleen was easily spooked, so Mal kept her call routine. The woman was nervous enough with the detail Mal had insisted stay on her and Jessi after Dodd made contact again.

At around eleven in the morning, Mal's lack of sleep, and perhaps a nasty bug, hit her hard.

She turned to Mike in the next cubicle, who was following up on a robbery from the week before. "I'm feeling like shit. You need anything, or can I leave early?"

"No problem. Go to the doctor. There's a nasty bug going around."

"Yeah, no thanks. I need some rest. Maybe some whiskey."

"Suit yourself. Just don't get me sick. Me and Gina are skydiving next weekend."

"You lose a bet?"

"It's one of Gina's bucket list things, and in a moment of stupidity, I agreed to go with her."

"Yeah, that *is* pretty fucking stupid. Well, it was nice knowing you. Make sure you leave me your record collection."

"My music would be wasted on you, *ABBA*."

"Hey, ABBA's the shit," Mal said, revisiting a common joke. Mike was anti-seventies pop, heavily into classic rock and jazz — or anything he thought of as *real music*.

"Yeah, I agree, ABBA *is* shit."

Mal grabbed her bag and got ready to go.

She stopped by Sheriff Bell's office to let her know she was leaving, but her boss was busy on the phone when Mal peeked in, probably talking to one of the council members trying to get on the right political side after the blowback of Councilman Conlan's recent scandal.

Conlan and the former sheriff, Claude Barry, had been strategizing ways to get Barry back into office in the coming November election. And Conlan had likely converted a few council members over to Barry's side. Conlan had been exposed as the perverted filth he was, his body found in a seedy Cuban hotel room along with a bunch of underage sex videos on his phone. Mal wondered if Mr. Parish knew anything about it.

The council had been forced to re-think their support for Barry, already saddled with the baggage of being a corrupt racist fuck. Mal hated the politics and wasn't sure how Sheriff Bell managed to maneuver through all of the bullshit.

Gloria looked up from her phone, saw Mal standing there, and waved.

Mal headed home for some drink and some shuteye.
Surely she'd feel better after a whiskey-soaked nap.

Chapter 3 - Mallory Black

MAL WOKE in her hotel room, where she'd been living for too long now, cell phone screaming on the nightstand.

Groggy from the cold medicine — and alcohol — she fumbled a bit before her fingers finally closed around the phone. Through sleep-blurred vision, she saw Mike's name and that it was only 11:05 PM.

What time did I go to bed?

"Yeah?"

"You okay?" he asked.

"Yeah, I'll be fine. Just need to sleep all weekend."

"Not talking about the flu. Talking about what's on TV."

She didn't like the sound of that. "What channel?"

"Any of them. All of them?"

Mal flipped on the local news and saw grainy footage of a woman outside a local dive bar. She was screaming at two men, then she punched one of them, followed by a kick to his ribs.

No, it wasn't *a* woman.

It was her.

"What the hell? When was this?"

The video went to a grainy shot of another, though similar, incident. Then it cut to Cameron Ford, the blogger who ran a gossip website disguised as news, talking to an interviewer.

"We held onto this a bit, even gave the sheriff an opportunity to handle it internally, but she refused. So we had to bring it to light."

Beneath him, the text read:

CREEK COUNTY DETECTIVE OUT OF CONTROL?

"And this isn't an isolated incident. We have four different videos of Detective Mallory Black engaged in conduct unbecoming law enforcement."

"Four videos? What were the first ones?" Mal asked Mike.

"Three fights, and one of you and some dude going at it in a car."

"What the fuck? This shit was from last year. Are they saying it's recent?"

"I don't think Ford gave dates, just 'the past year.' I think they're alluding to this happening while you were with the department. My guess is they've had a P.I. following you for a while, saving their hits for just before the election. Did Sheriff Bell come to you with any of this?"

"No!"

Mal seethed, staring at the troublemaking blogger, working against the public interest to manufacture propaganda for the former sheriff, who was doing whatever he could to win his seat back in November.

Mallory thought Ford would've had the decency to slink away after his actions led to an angry lynch mob causing the tragic death of an innocent man not even a

month ago. But clearly he had no soul. He kept spewing his bullshit into the camera.

"What we have here is the tip of the iceberg from a long investigation into the Creek County Sheriff's Department. More videos are coming into our Citizens for Responsible Law Enforcement website, regular people like you and me, fed up with the wild-west style of Sheriff Bell's regime."

The news anchor, who didn't ask who was funding this so-called "investigation" or argue that she might not have been one of those "regular people," threw him a softball.

"And you offered the sheriff a chance to take care of this. How did Sheriff Bell respond?"

Ford laughed. "She's ignored all of my emails and calls. Detective Mallory Black has *personally* threatened me on several occasions."

Mal turned off the TV in disgust. "He's a fucking liar!"

"Did you threaten him?"

Her phone beeped. Mallory pulled it from her ear to see who was calling.

Sheriff Bell.

"Hold on. Gloria's on the other line." She clicked over. "I'm guessing you're enjoying some TV?"

"What is this?"

"It's nothing. They're desperate, looking for shit on me to get to you. Stupid bar fights with assholes who deserved it. Yes, all of them. They either started shit with me or other women in the bar. Not a single one has tried to sue me."

"Well, that in itself is a small miracle, I suppose."

"Because they knew they were fucking wrong. And so is Cameron Ford. It's a hit piece, and you know it."

"What else might they have?"

Gloria wasn't going to come out and acknowledge

25

Mal's struggle with pain killers, not on a phone where someone might be listening. Or recording.

"They've got nothing else," Mal assured her, before launching into a violent fit of coughing.

She grabbed a bottle of water from her nightstand and drank. Her throat was still raw.

Gloria was quiet for a long moment, probably trying to figure out how this would blow up on her Monday morning. The good news, if there was any, was that it happened on a Friday. Surprising since the weekend's edge was when companies buried bad news in hopes that it'd vanish before Sunday dinner.

But maybe that was a good move. Gloria probably wouldn't respond with a press conference until Monday, meaning it'd push the bad news right back into next week's headlines. This was Creek County, where bad news had a way of gaining fuel over time until it burned everyone in its path.

Small Florida towns had a way of stoking the drama to keep it alive.

"I need to put you on paid administrative leave," Gloria said.

"What? Over videos from a year ago, when I didn't even work for the department?"

"Listen, Mal, I know you had a rough time after Ashley died. And you're still not good. I have the utmost faith in you, I do. But appearances are everything, and we need to at least look like we're investigating the matter. We're under a microscope after the Burridge incident, like never before. Give me a week or so. Then we can say we looked into it, found nothing worthwhile, and clear your name."

"Burridge? The situation *they* created by instigating a witch hunt and a lynch mob against an innocent man? You're playing defense, Sheriff. And that means you're

letting Barry dictate the game. You're better than that. This is them trying to reposition the argument after their boy Conlan went down. Ignore it."

"I'm sorry, Mal. I suggest you talk with your union rep and lay low until this blows over."

Gloria hung up.

Mal clicked back over to Mike and sighed. "Well, I'm on leave, partner."

"Damn it. Sorry. Anything I can do?"

"Tell me why I shouldn't go find that fucking blogger and kick *his* ass?"

"Obviously, that's a terrible idea."

She coughed again. "I couldn't now if I wanted to. All right, I'm going to wallow in misery for a few days."

"Call me if you need me."

"Thanks, Mike."

Mal hung up and turned on the TV, flipping channels until she found someone discussing this bullshit. She felt violated as she watched grainy footage of her in a car on top of a man. Maybe, in the strictest sense of the word, it wasn't an invasion of privacy — she had been in public — but it sure as hell felt like slut shaming, anyway.

Hey, look at this woman having random sex in front of a seedy-ass bar!

And she did feel shame.

Not for the random sex. But for allowing herself to get so out of control, to be so self-destructive.

How she could have been so blind to the darkness, missed how bad things had gotten? How bad they could still be had she not been pulled back onto the force to help save another little girl taken by the man who murdered her daughter.

While Mal and Jasper might have saved Jessi, in many ways, Jessi had saved her.

She had given Mal a reason to care again. A reason to fight the darkness instead of surrendering to it. A reason to stop taking the pills.

Jessi reminded Mal that she could still do good in the world and put bad men like Dodd away.

And that gave her purpose.

But now Cameron, Barry, and whoever else was in their little circle of influence were trying to take that all away — to get her fired.

She hated them for standing in her way. For preventing her from doing her fucking job.

As Mal watched video of her punching then kicking some asshole, she wondered who had been following her and filming this. Had it been different people catching her drunken, drugged behavior on camera, or had Conlan, Barry, or Ford hired some asshole to follow her?

And if someone was following her, what else did they see? Her abusing drugs? Her leaving a Narcotics Anonymous meeting? What other videos might drop? And might they prevent her from ever returning to the department?

Mal didn't care. Whatever else they might have, she wouldn't let these people lurking in the shadows prevent her from doing good in this world. She'd lost too much time wallowing in self-pity after Ashley died.

She couldn't pause her war with the darkness.

But then the coughing came to claim her. *Maybe just a few minutes.*

Sunday, August 25

Chapter 4 - Paul Dodd

PAUL LAY in the cold on a little mat, reading a book from the library, passing time until dinner. A history book about pre-war Germany. He had no interest in Germany, but he'd already read most of the other history books. He'd also read the social science books, most of them dog-eared copies from the eighties and nineties. Even a few lame thrillers. Getting any romances was almost impossible. They were gold in jail.

He was in the D Wing, or Delta Three, as the guards called it. High security, where they stashed the murderers and rapists. Paul was both. Being a county jail, there weren't many murderers locked up awaiting trial. There were a dozen cells in this housing unit, but only two people occupied them now — Paul and an older Hispanic man named Hector. There had been three, but Danny got sent off to the state penitentiary last week.

He'd been Paul's favorite. Danny knew everything about the jail, the hierarchies, and how to work the system. Not that it did him much good, since Paul was so isolated. But Danny had given him excellent advice about

surviving prison once he was likely found guilty and sent there.

And Danny knew how to get shit done.

He was the one who facilitated the whole delivery system to send videos to Mallory and Jessi's mother. With him gone, Paul wondered if the delivery guy could be trusted not to ransack the storage unit where Paul stored the videos, maybe even contact the authorities or some media outlet that would pay for such a prize.

Those videos were his trophies. All he had left of his time with the girls.

And now they might all be gone.

Why?

Because he'd used them to bargain with Mallory for a visit.

Not his proudest moment.

He hated himself for being so weak, so lonely, that he just had to get her to visit.

Paul had never been much of a people person, never imagined that he'd mind being alone. But the forced isolation of prison was predator to the prey of his senses.

He was so desperate for any communication, he looked forward to spending time with Hector and his broken English. Hell, he even enjoyed talking to the few guards who didn't treat him like a pariah.

While Paul awaited trial, he sometimes wondered if he'd be better off pleading guilty just so he could get on with it. He had zero hope of winning his freedom. *Maybe* they'd find him crazy enough to throw him in a psychiatric facility.

But if he failed, he'd wind up at a state prison. Which, according to Danny, wasn't nearly as bad as the county jail. Because in prison you had more freedom. And you weren't alone in a max security wing. If you behaved yourself, you

could have physical visitations instead of the Plexiglas-and-phone bullshit.

Not that anyone, other than his lawyer, would ever visit Paul.

He was dead to his ex-wife and daughter. He got Mallory to visit, but that hadn't gone well. Despite his promises of additional videos showing her Ashley's dying days, the detective would not be returning. Maybe she would make it back to watch him die.

So it was just him and Hector.

On the rare occasions when they got rec time together in the day room, they didn't talk much. Sometimes they'd watch TV. Other times, they'd play chess. Hector was decent enough, but not exactly a challenge to his intellect. Paul would sometimes handicap his game, make a few bad moves, sacrifice a powerful piece to make things more interesting. Sometimes Hector won, which gave him the juice to play more and Paul a little delight in seeing the man working to improve his game.

But today Hector wasn't at rec time. He was in the sick ward, so Paul sat alone watching TV. A *Golden Girls* episode, something he had never seen on the outside. But even *Golden Girls* was worth watching in jail.

Then aired the commercial for that cruise line with the little girl in a skimpy bathing suit. Oil for his pistons later.

Still, Paul would've preferred playing chess to being alone.

As much as he hated the loneliness of six months in what more or less amounted to solitary confinement, Paul was glad not to be in gen pop. One guard, a big black dude named Lawrence, told him to stop griping about being bored and to thank his fucking stars he wasn't in gen pop.

A kiddy-diddler winds up there, he gets his wig split.

A buzzing outside drew his attention.

Paul put his book down, stood, then went to his window, hoping to see Hector. It was too late for rec time today, but maybe he could play chess tomorrow.

But it wasn't Hector.

Two guards were shoving a big bald white dude with a swastika on his giant neck toward the cell next to Paul's. He was holding a new arrival's plastic tub — a mat, blanket, pillow, cup with toothpaste, and plastic spoon.

As they passed his door, the man glared at Paul through the window.

And though he had never seen him before, there was the briefest glint of recognition in the man's eyes before he was out of view and being led into his cell.

Paul settled back on his bed and tried to read.

After a while, the silence was shattered by his new neighbor, moving around, and eventually, seemingly, throwing his shit against the wall. Then he began shouting, "Fuck!" over and over.

Paul wondered if the guards were going to silence him.

He even got up to peer through his window, up at the control room on the second story looking down on the day room and the housing block. But nobody seemed to be making a move.

Paul wanted to tell the man to shut up, but the guy was a giant who could easily "split his wig." Didn't want that, so he stayed quiet.

Monday, August 26

Chapter 5 - Paul Dodd

HECTOR WAS BACK the next day.

The doors opened, then he and Paul entered the day room, a circular space with a quadrant of tables and chairs bolted to the floor, a TV up high where they couldn't reach it, and a water fountain.

The new man's door buzzed open, but he didn't step out.

Hector looked at the cell door, then at Paul. "Who's he?"

"I don't know. We haven't been introduced." Then, he whispered, "I think he's a Nazi."

"Great. Just what we need in here, a fucking Nazi," Hector said, way too loud.

Paul glanced at the door, afraid the man would come barreling out and unleash on them.

Hector was surely a badass in his youth, but Paul wasn't sure how tough the old man was now. He'd been in the sick ward yesterday puking his guts out. And Paul wasn't much of a fighter, at least not against someone so large.

But more than anything, he wanted to avoid situations that would affect his rec time. He'd lost it twice — once for something Danny had done and another time after the incident with Mallory's visit, when he lost his shit.

Losing rec time wasn't a one-day punishment. The guards stole a week at a time.

And a week without rec, stuck in your cell, except shower times, was about as close to hell as Paul hoped to ever get.

Hector set the chess pieces onto squares etched into the metal table. "You ready to lose today, friend?"

"Oh, did you suddenly learn how to play in the sick ward?"

The old man's laugh collapsed into a ragged cough.

Three minutes in, Hector had lost three pawns and a knight. Paul was down one intentional pawn.

The door opened behind them.

Paul turned to see the Nazi step out. He was taller, wider, and more muscular than the giant he seemed to be in passing the day before.

He glared at them with bloodshot blue eyes. To Paul he said, "Why you playing with that spic, brother?"

His shaved head must've made him look like a fellow believer in genocide.

Hector stood. "Whatchyou say, bitch?"

The Nazi started toward Hector.

Paul, without even thinking, stood between them. "Hey, hey, if you two throw punches, the guards are going to come in here and beat us all. Then we'll lose rec for a week."

The two men glared at one another, neither wanting to retreat.

"Come on," Paul said, meeting the Nazi's icy eyes,

"we're all in this shit together. Just three of us in this wing. No need to choose sides."

The Nazi snorted, turned from the fight, then sat at the table with the remote, looking for something to watch.

But now Hector didn't want to play. His pride was wounded, and he was itching for a fight.

Paul sat back down. "Come on. Your move, Hector. You going to let me win this shit?"

He turned to Paul, glanced at the Nazi, then back at Paul before he finally sat.

They played for a while as the Nazi flipped between news channels, muttering about all the races he didn't like "taking over the fucking TV." After a few minutes, he said, "You that Paul Dodd guy?"

Paul and Hector traded looks.

In all their months together, Hector had never once asked Paul about what he was in for. Paul appreciated that. Danny had asked, but the guy had also never judged him.

Paul couldn't help but feel that the Nazi, of all fucking people, might take issue with his crimes.

"Yeah." He didn't bother to look back.

Never show fear, Danny had said. *Fear is putting a target on your back. You did what you did. Own it. People will either respect you or fear you. But don't be timid, or they will make you their bitch.*

Paul's bishop took Hector's queen.

"Fuck," Hector said.

The Nazi came over to their table.

Paul tried to show no fear, but hell if his heart wasn't hammering, anyway.

Hector, despite having had words with the Nazi, also didn't appear particularly nervous. He probably played his cards closer to the vest.

Paul glanced up at the control booth wondering how long it would take for the guards to intervene. Hell, they'd

probably need to call in backup for Goliath. Paul would probably be shivved in the back by then.

Danny once told him about a snitch he watched get taken down in the rec area outside. Five seconds, forty-five stab wounds. Dude was dead before the guards saw him hit the ground.

The Nazi said, "He's got you in four moves, *esé*."

Hector ignored the sarcasm, and made his next move, surrendering a pawn to protect his last bishop.

Paul took the pawn and cleared the way for him to bring his queen down the board and close ranks. Another three moves, and Hector was done.

"You play?" Paul asked the Nazi.

"You could say that."

Paul wondered what *that* meant. Was he some sort of grand champion?

"Want to play the winner next match?" Paul asked.

"Nah, I'll just watch for now."

He took a seat between them at the circular table. His elbows on the table took up enough space to provoke Hector. But he ignored the infringement, focused on the game, probably realizing he was indeed running out of viable moves. Paul's pieces were lined up perfectly and Hector's only moves were staving off the inevitable loss.

Paul loved these moments, watching his opponents' options narrow and the realization darken their eyes. But he found it hard to enjoy today's game, studied as he was by their new pod mate.

Paul won in four moves, as predicted. "Good game," he said as Hector sighed.

The Nazi snorted. "Yeah, good game, for a dirty spic."

Hector lost his veneer of control and took a swing.

The Nazi was fast, more so than any human Paul had ever seen. He reached up and grabbed Hector by his neck,

lifted him up, then slammed him down to the ground. And then the giant pummeled him.

Paul was frozen in indecision, looking up to see if the guards had seen anything, if they were moving in. If not, the fucker might kill Hector.

Paul had to act, but what the hell could he do against this behemoth?

Another bit of early Danny advice, *When you're in with a crew, you ride with that group when shit goes down.* Loyalty meant everything behind bars. Betray your crew, get fucked.

Hector's face was a bloody mess. His nose broken. And the Nazi wasn't letting up.

Paul reached out and grabbed his fist. "Stop!"

He spun around, his eyes boring in on Paul's, a vicious smile claiming his face.

Time froze as Paul stared at the giant and his certain death.

But then the doors buzzed open behind them.

Guards rushed in.

He froze, raising his hands as if he'd been caught in similar predicaments a hundred times before.

The guards wrestled him down then cuffed him.

The Nazi stared up at Paul, smiling.

∾

Tuesday, August 27

Chapter 6 - Paul Dodd

THE NEXT DAY Paul had the wing to himself.

Hector was in the medical ward and the Nazi, whose name Paul still didn't know, was in solitary.

Rec time was another day of TV alone. But he couldn't focus with his eyes always drifting back to the scene of their battle. Guards had bleached the blood from the floor and table, but a part of Paul still sensed it there, invisible but to him.

A reminder of just how vicious this place could be. How life could end in a second.

He wondered if the Nazi would be returned to his cell. And if so, had Paul made an enemy in trying to protect Hector?

Choose your enemies wisely. Because nobody forgets anything in here.

He felt sick to his stomach. Why the hell did Hector have to take a swing? Why couldn't he just let shit go?

He never understood the overinflated sense of pride that street thugs and prisoners seemed to have. Guys like

that took offense at the slightest perceived insult. For a bunch of toughs, they were the biggest bitches he'd ever seen. Not that *he'd* ever say that to any of them.

Paul knew he where he was in the food chain. And how to swim clear of the sharks.

Chapter 7 - Paul Dodd

AFTER DINNER, Paul was led to the showers in a connected concrete room with chain link running the long wall for stalls.

Typically, he and Hector would shower in their own cage at the same time while a guard kept watch, just in case one of them got to thinking about killing or fucking.

Danny had told Paul that this was one of the benefits of the showers in the Delta Wing over other areas of the jail and state prisons, where you were more likely to be showering with other dudes and anything could happen.

Vic, one of the surly guards that was never, ever, talkative, stood near the door, waiting for Paul to finish. He didn't much care for showering in front of others, always feeling as though they were staring at the scars on his back, permanent gifts from his mother. After a while, he had learned to block them all out. He did his business, dried off, got dressed, and returned to his cell.

He finished rinsing the shampoo from his hair, turned the water off, then turned to open the cage.

But something was wrong.

The guard wasn't in his spot near the door.

Instead, the Nazi was standing there, smiling.

Don't show fear.

Paul nodded, grabbed his towel off the sink, and wrapped it around his waist.

"Hey, you get out early?"

"Tell me, Paul, did you enjoy fucking those little girls?"

Shit.

He froze in front of the sinks, trying not to look like the cornered animal he was. Wanting to grab his orange jumpsuit and put it on, as if it could serve as armor for what was to come.

Where the fuck is the guard?

"What's it like, that ten-year-old pussy? I bet it's nice and tight, eh?"

Paul wasn't sure if the man was a fan of his work or disgusted by it. Nor did he know what answer might spare him.

The Nazi stalked toward him, stood just six feet from Paul, blocking his escape.

"I asked you a question. Were they tight?"

"I don't remember."

"Bullshit. How do you forget a thing like that? I wouldn't! Sweet little hairless slits. Well, I don't know. Do ten year olds have hair? What with girls maturing so fast these days, who knows? Well, you do, eh? So, tell me, Paul, do they have hair?"

Okay, maybe he is a fan.

"I dunno."

"But you do remember, don't you?"

"Um …"

Before Paul could stammer out his next words, the Nazi rushed him, his hand extended.

Then it was around Paul's throat, shoving him hard into the chain link fence.

Paul tried to scream, but the Nazi said, "Shhh … You don't scream, I won't kill you. Deal?"

Gasping for air, Paul nodded as best he could with the man's vice-like grip.

"Okay, here's what's gonna happen. I'm going to ease up, just enough for you to talk, okay?"

Paul nodded.

"And then you're gonna tell me a story. Tell me what it was like fucking one of those girls. And I want details."

Paul was confused. "What?"

"Fucking tell me a story. And make it hot."

Nazi Fuck slipped out of his overalls, dropping them to the ground, stroking his already hard cock.

What the fuck is happening?

Before Paul could process anything more, the Nazi barked, "Talk!"

Paul began to talk about one of the girls.

"Describe what she was wearing."

Paul did.

As he spilled details one of the girls, a girl named Rebecca, the Nazi stroked harder and faster, closing his eyes. "Did she have hair?"

What the hell was his thing about pubic hair?

"No."

"Ohhh," said the Nazi.

Paul hoped the fucker would leave once he came.

"Tell me how tight she was."

As disgusted as Paul was at what was happening, his arousal could not be ignored. He wasn't sure if it was from this naked man jerking it next to him, or if he was turned on by thoughts of Rebecca. Either way, a part of Paul hoped the man might go down on him. Or ask him to.

"She was real tight." Paul watched the man's face redden as he stroked his dick faster.

He thought of Wes, the man who had groomed him and his sister.

The only man that Paul had ever thought of sexually, until now.

Getting sucked off by a skinhead wasn't the type of sex he wanted, but in prison, any contact was something.

The Nazi's eyes were still closed as he reached down and grabbed Paul's cock, and began to stroke him, never letting go of himself.

Paul came immediately.

And once he was done, the Nazi opened his eyes. That smile returned to his face.

"How tight was she?"

He had to continue the story, though Paul was no longer aroused. "Real tight."

"No, I want you to *show* me."

"What?"

Paul never saw the fist coming until his jaw exploded, and his teeth chattered on the ground.

He followed them to the floor.

"What the fuck?" Paul cried out, though his throbbing mouth warped every word.

And the Nazi was on top of him, straddling him, his weight like a mountain.

Hands around Paul's neck, squeezing tight, pushing his face into the ground, harder.

Oh God, no!

"Was she *this* tight?" He thrust himself into Paul.

Paul screamed.

Wednesday, August 28

Chapter 8 - Mallory Black

MAL WOKE up with a five-alarm hangover.

You weren't supposed to drink while taking the good syrup, and she had. Her tax was a headache that echoed in her bones.

But at least her throat wasn't screaming And she didn't wake up coughing her guts out.

Maybe she was finally improving.

After spending most of the past five days living on room service, she'd have to finally venture outdoors and face the media that was wanting some response in the wake of her being put on leave. Her phone had blown up, so she stopped answering calls. Mike and her ex-husband, Ray, had her private number if they wanted to talk. Everyone else could fuck off.

She crawled out of bed and grabbed both of her phones on the way to the bathroom. She hadn't showered in two, maybe three, days.

She drew a hot bath, got inside, and started checking messages, work phone first. Seventy-three unanswered calls.

She laughed and put the phone down.

Then she went to her personal phone, surprised to find three messages. Two from Mike and one from a number she didn't recognize.

"Hey, it's Mike. Jessi Price has been taken. And the deputy we put on her is dead. Sheriff needs you to call her."

Mal froze.

Oh, my God. Jessi is gone?

Her fingers trembled, but she pressed *Play* on the second message anyway.

Mike again. "Where are you, Mal? If you're not gonna call her, then at least get back to me. I need to know if you have anything. Also, Jessi's mom has been calling your work number. But you should talk to Gloria first."

Mal got out of the bath, did a half-assed job of drying off, then walked into the living room and flipped on the news while dialing Gloria.

She picked up immediately. "Where the hell are you?"

"Um, you put me on leave, remember?"

"What did Paul Dodd say to you?"

"What?"

"When you went to meet him in jail. What did he say that made you request a detail?"

"It wasn't what he said. It was that he had someone working with him, to deliver videos to me and to Colleen Price. I already told you all this. Do you think his accomplice did this?"

"I don't know. If so, he had more than one. An armed man in a ski mask driving a van got in front of her school bus, boarded, then shot and killed the driver. He threw Jessi in a van and took off. Deputy Siegel moved in to intercept but was shot and killed by another suspect. Reports of

at least three men, all wearing ski masks and dressed in black."

"Is Dodd still in jail?"

"Yes, verified. In fact, he was brutally assaulted yesterday and is in the medical ward now."

"Brutalized? Beaten, or?"

"Beaten and raped by some Nazi. We're trying to get to the bottom of this, see if there's any connection. We're also talking to everyone who's been in contact with Dodd since his lockup."

"There's gotta be a connection. He and Jessi are attacked at around the same time …"

She thought about Jasper's warnings — that Dodd would escape and get Jessi again. She thought about telling Gloria, but what good would that do? If she hadn't managed to locate Jasper, neither would anyone else. And right now, he was the only one who seemed to have any helpful information. If Mal told Gloria about the warnings, she would tell the Feds. Jasper would vanish, and she might never find Jessi again.

"Bring me back, Sheriff. I can help find her."

"Sorry, Mal. You know I can't do that. Plus, the Feds are involved, so everything's got to be above board. But if you can think of anything, or if anyone reaches out to you, please call me immediately."

"Anything I need to know before I call Colleen?"

"No. I think she just needs some reassurance that her girl will be okay. That we'll find her."

"Got it."

Gloria said goodbye, then hung up.

Mal stared at the phone trying to decide if she should return Mike's call or listen to her voicemails.

Her work phone rang.

PRIVATE NUMBER.

She picked up.

"You should've listened to me," Jasper said.

"I *did* listen to you. We already had a detail on her. And Paul is in jail. This wasn't him."

"It wasn't?" Pure surprise thickened his voice.

"No. He is still in jail. Got beat up pretty bad, from what I hear. This was men in ski masks, at least three."

"*Three?* I didn't see that on the news. They said one man. Ah, of course, they're keeping that part private to weed the tipsters from the cranks."

"You were a cop, you know how it goes. Listen, we need to talk, in person."

"I'm not coming in."

"Please, just to clear some things."

"Yeah, right. And then you're asking me about Wes and Calum. No thanks, Detective."

"I'm not looking to hook you for those things. I just want Jessi back."

"I don't see how us talking in person will help you. I'd suggest you do as I said and have someone take care of Dodd, before he's gone."

"He's not going anywhere."

"Yeah, we'll see about that." Then Jasper hung up.

"Fuck!" Mal dropped her phone on the sofa, went back to the bathroom, finished washing up, then got dressed.

She needed to be working this case. Living on the front lines. If anyone could find Jessi again, it would be her.

She wished Cameron Ford was in the bar downstairs. It was his fault she was on leave. Him and his stupid gotcha videos. She wondered how long he'd been holding onto them. Probably months. Was likely waiting to hit the sheriff closer to election.

Part of her wished she could run into him now, while

on leave. She imagined walking up to him, punching him in the face, then kicking him in the balls.

Get that *on film, you fuck!*

Yes, she'd never work again. And he would probably sue her, but every dime would be worth it — at least for the few minutes she'd be watching him bleed.

Mal braced herself for the next call, to Colleen. She wanted a pill to ease the tightening vice on her skull. But she needed a clear head. Mal might not be on the job, but she would do everything she could as a private citizen, and Colleen might be the best way to stay in the game. Mal could offer her services, pro bono, as a consultant. That would keep her close to the case, maybe allow her to get some vital piece of information.

She dialed, her mind flashing back to the night when Dodd had tried to rape Jessi right in front of her. The girl's terrified eyes, how she looked to her for help. But Mal had been helpless, restrained on the bed, and forced to watch. They would have both died that night if not for Jasper Parish.

Could he be counted on to come through again?

Mal couldn't be certain, and so it wasn't worth the chance.

For now, she had only herself and the will to save Jessi.

Somehow. Some way.

Chapter 9 - Paul Dodd

PAUL LAY in the medical ward wishing he were dead.

The Nazi had raped, beat, and nearly killed him before a guard had finally come and pulled the behemoth away.

There wasn't a part of him not in pain. The doc said they'd given him painkillers while he was out, probably only the minimum dosage. He was a monster, after all. A rapist and murderer of children. Why not give him a taste of the pain he surely deserved?

Paul vaguely remembered being brought into the medical ward. After that, he blacked out until this morning.

He also half-recalled his conversation with Dr. Blanc, a short old Jewish man who looked like he last practiced in the Old West. The doc informed him he was lucky he didn't suffer anal tearing. That would've required stitching and left him in even more pain. Apparently, the Nazi wasn't particularly well-endowed, or had gone easy on Paul — thank God for small miracles.

But his face, ribs, and back felt pummeled by batons. In time, that pain would fade. But the psychological effects of

his assault would linger much longer. Fortunately, the doc said, they had a great psychologist on staff who would start therapy with Paul in the morning to help him deal with the trauma.

Fuck the psychologist, I want more meds.

As Paul stared at the glass door of his medical wing cell, he wondered how many of the guards in the control booth just outside his door were in on what happened to him.

Vic, the guard who had left him in the shower alone, had obviously known the Nazi was going to rape him. It was surely arranged ahead of time. But how deep did the plan run, and would anyone hold the guard accountable? Probably not. Guards and prison authorities protected their own.

Another question bubbled to the surface. *Did Mallory give the order?*

He'd heard stories of corrupt cops reaching out and striking at prisoners they felt had somehow escaped a harsh enough sentence. And who better to use as an instrument than a giant Nazi rapist fuck?

He flashed back to Mal blowing up at him during her visit. From the other side of the Plexiglas, she said, "If you ever fuck with the Price family again — so much as wave in their general direction or send one of your buddies to deliver a message —it will become my mission to find new and inventive ways to make you wish I'd let you die."

Was this what she'd meant?

Had his delivery person sent another video to Jessi ahead of schedule or reached out to the girl?

And was this her revenge? To order him beaten and raped?

Paul wished he'd killed Mal when he'd had the chance.

Hell, he'd had two — once when he watched over her as she slept, and another when he'd taken her.

Should've left well enough alone. Should've just left with Jessi. Why did he have to bring Mal back to her house? What the hell had he been thinking?

He couldn't understand his fascination with Mallory. Her daughter, Ashley, hadn't even been his favorite girl. But as time passed, something about her stayed with him.

His regret was killing her when he did. Not keeping her around. He wouldn't be in this predicament if he had.

Sure, she would've gotten older, developed breasts, and grown unattractive, turning into a despicable shrew like all little girls eventually did. But maybe he could've learned to love her, to be aroused by an adolescent. Perhaps he could've short-circuited that bitchy teenage period and taught her to stay young and sweet forever.

As if time could be stopped.

But it wasn't just about her appearance, as beautiful as she was. No, there was also an extra element of excitement in Ashley being a detective's daughter. It his first truly valuable target.

Most of the kids had been nothings, practically discarded by society.

But not Ashley. Her mother was part of an untouchable class.

And he found that excitement again when he took Jessi, especially after Mal got involved.

Fucking with Mal brought him immeasurable pleasure, though he'd spent many nights trying to understand why.

Was he reliving his time with Ashley through her? Maybe in part, but there was something else, too. Something he couldn't quite figure out, an anger he felt when considering what a shitty mother she was — a drunk who'd

become a drug addict, divorced, and too busy with her job to properly care for her kid.

She was pathetic. And after the news of her daughter's death came out, she was all over the news, crying and whining, like she actually cared about Ashley.

Had she been a good mother, Ashley would have never appeared on Paul's radar.

She invited this upon herself. And then, because apparently shitty mothers always wound up on top, she won the fucking lottery a year later.

That *really* pissed him off.

So taking Jessi, a girl that could've passed for Ashley's sister, had excited him, almost as much as Ashley herself.

And while Jessi had quickly proved to be a little bitch, Paul still wished they could've spent more time together.

Under different circumstances, she might have learned to have loved him.

But no. He'd been stupid, pursuing that cunt Mallory Black instead of appreciating what he had.

And now he was suffering.

He wondered if this was only the beginning. If the guards would make this routine, *accidentally* leaving him alone with a rapist. If so, how many times would it happen before they finally decided to kill him?

Paul wished Mallory had killed him. She'd had the chance. But the detective was twisted by a need to hurt him.

It was kind of funny, in a dark way — two people braided by a desire to hurt one another.

The guards were moving around outside his door. Paul wondered if they were coming to usher him back to his regular cell. God, he hoped not. He wasn't ready to be away from the meds.

The door opened to a tall man with slicked back hair,

an expensive suit, and wireframe glasses. He looked like a doctor, or—

"Hello, Mr. Dodd, my name is Lawrence Kampf." He held out his hand. "I'm your new attorney."

"New attorney?" Paul repeated, confused, shaking the man's hand.

"I'll be taking over your case." He turned to the guards. "Can my client and I have some privacy, please?"

The two guards traded a look, then left.

"What happened? Did the other guy give up on me?" Death row was like breath on his neck.

Kampf smiled. "*Give up on you?*" The lawyer laughed as if Paul was missing something obvious. After a moment of waiting for him to get it, he said, "I'm not a public defender, Mr. Dodd. I'm with Wallace, Kampf, and Goldman. We're the best representation you could ever hope to get."

"Best? Who's paying for this?"

"I'm glad you asked. Your friend, Wes Richardson? He left you a sizable estate."

"Define sizable."

"Fifteen million and change."

Paul gasped, then launched into a coughing fit that felt like blades slicing into his ribs.

Spittle of blood coated his lips.

"We're going to get you transferred to a facility that will actually protect you, then I'm launching a suit against the sheriff's office and the jail for allowing this to happen. You can expect that fortune to increase."

Paul stared in disbelief, tears welling up in his eyes. He had so many questions, chief among them was why Wes left him a fortune. Also, now that he had money, could his victims attack the assets?

"Thank you," Paul said.

Kampf pulled out his cell phone and aimed the camera. "Now look miserable. Like you're dying, in as much pain as possible. These photos will play well at trial."

Paul didn't have to try. He stared into the camera and wondered if things might finally turn around.

Could this man actually get him off?

Chapter 10 - Mallory Black

MAL PULLED up to the Holiday Inn where Colleen was placed after Jessi's abduction — just in case Dodd, someone working with him, or a copycat, had designs to murder her mom like Paul had done to her father.

She spoke briefly with the deputy standing outside Colleen's room, then was ushered in.

Colleen was sitting at a desk, eyes glued to the local 24-hour news station, which had quickly become Jessi Price Central, updating viewers with every tiny detail, and talking to anyone, no matter how trivial the person or their thoughts. Eyes and nose red, clenching a fistful of tissue, she looked at Mal. "I should've never let her go back to school."

When Mal hugged her, Colleen squeezed as if she were the only thing anchoring her to a world where Jessi still lived and keeping her from drifting off to that other place where a grieving parent found no solace. A place she would probably never return from.

"It's not your fault," Mal said when Colleen eventually let her go.

"No, it is. I should've kept her home, or hell, moved to Kentucky with my sister. Got the hell away from all these terrible memories."

She sat back in her chair, eyes on the TV as if someone might break with news that Jessi was safe.

Mal sat opposite her on one of the two beds. "The sheriff's office and the FBI are doing everything they can to find Jessi. She *will* be okay."

"I'd feel better if you were on the case."

"I'm on leave right now, but I'll do everything I can. I'm sure you've already told the detectives everything, but is there anything you remember that might help find her? Any people or vehicles you saw around."

"No one stuck out. I figured with the detail you had on us, everything was fine. You know? It's so awful what happened to that officer. Did … did he have a family?"

"He wasn't married. No kids. And yes, it's tragic."

"If they can kill a sheriff deputy that easily, what hope does Jessi have? Do you think …" Colleen swallowed. "Do you think Paul Dodd has anything to do with this?"

"We're looking into every possibility."

Even though she wasn't part of the *we* in this instance, it was a habit to say the thing that most kept hope alive. But Mal wasn't lying. The sheriff's office and the FBI would be doing everything possible to find her. This was quickly elevated to a high priority case because of the deputy's murder as well as the target — someone who had already been kidnapped and subjected to Dodd's horror show.

Colleen stared at the TV. "You know, it's funny. After Jessi came home, I was paranoid about every person we ran into. Everyone was a potential predator, from people we passed on the street to the old man four doors down. It took me forever to lower my guard, to let her back in

school. To let her take the bus so she wouldn't feel like a freak. And just when I learned to relax a little, someone does this."

She closed her eyes, fresh tears streaming down her cheeks. "Did you ever go and talk to ... *him*?"

"I hadn't intended to," Mal said. "But when he started using you to get to me, I didn't have any choice."

"And? What did he want?"

"For me to keep visiting. He promised to give me more videos of Ashley's last days. Acted like he was doing me a favor. Like I wanted to see my daughter's final terrified moments."

"What did you say?"

"I told him no." Mal shook her head, not bothering to explain how she also threatened the man to stay away from Jessi, lest he suffer. She wished she'd kept her temper under better control and hated to think her threat may have led to what happened this morning.

"Did he seem okay with that? Like he was going to stop bothering you?"

"I think so," Mal said.

"Has anyone spoken to him about this yet?"

"I'm sure."

"But you don't know. And you haven't spoken to him?"

"Well, there's a complication. He's in the medical ward. Someone attacked him, hurt him badly enough that he was unconscious. I'm sure my partner will be talking to him as soon as he can."

Colleen's shoulders slumped. "I can't do this again. The not knowing if she's okay. The waiting. It's ... too much. I feel like there's something I should be doing! My daughter is out there while I'm just sitting in here, watching TV. That's not what a parent's supposed to do."

"I know the feeling."

Mal wanted to add that it was even harder for her, because detectives are supposed to solve cases. Yet she couldn't even find her own daughter before it was too late.

But this wasn't a competition in who felt more useless. Nor would it inspire confidence in Colleen.

So Mal put a hand on her shoulder. "We'll find her."

Chapter 11 - Jasper Parish

Jasper stared at the television, frozen on an image of the bus, the masked man grabbing Jessi and dragging her off at gunpoint, while frightened children looked on helplessly. A kid had filmed it, but didn't know anything when questioned, other than how to record.

Jordyn sat beside him on the couch. "How many times are you going to watch this?"

"There's something there. Don't you see it? Can't you *feel* something?"

She got off the couch and sat closer to the TV. "Okay, play it again."

He did, and they stared at the screen, waiting for the inscrutable to start making sense.

"What's that?"

He paused and rewound the video. "What?" He saw nothing new in the jiggly camerawork of a scared child with a cell phone.

"Slow it down when you see the redhead kid stand."

The redhead with the blue shirt stood. Jasper slowed the video, and the screen lurched forward at a few frames

per second. It was harder to make sense of anything when the video moved so slowly. Everything seemed fuzzier, objects lost clarity, and there were several instances of the screen going dark as the kid recording the video moved to either hide or get a better angle.

"Rewind again. Hit pause when it goes dark, then advance one frame at a time until it goes light."

Jasper followed her orders, his aging eyes narrowing in on the TV and straining to see whatever his teenage daughter might have picked up on.

"There!"

He paused the frame, and titled his head, trying to make sense of what he was seeing.

"It's out the window. Near the van. That guy."

Jasper got off the couch, moved next to his daughter, and crouched down.

The image was fuzzy, and the man was wearing a mask, but his frame seemed *very* familiar. A giant of a man whose silhouette was instantly recognizable, even standing in a blurry background. Something insisting in his brain, that same thing that had screamed and been right so many times before.

"No, it can't be him. That doesn't make any sense."

"Who is it?" Jordyn asked.

"His name is Cadillac Taylor, an enforcer for a crime family in South Florida. Built like a shit brick house. Dude was chasing down people that owed his boss, Lil' Tony, money. He was scaring away the competition, not kidnapping children."

"Do you know where he is now?"

"Cadillac vanished when Lil' Tony got gunned down at some nightclub in South Beach. Local cops didn't know if he got out of Dodge because Tony's boss, Curtis Johnson, blamed him, or if someone popped him, too."

"Do you know where he is now?"

"No, but I know someone who might."

"It's him, isn't it?" Jasper said, looking at his old friend, Lenny Barnes.

"Sure looks like him. I mean, as much as someone can with a mask on. But that's his shape. Damned shame what happened to him, such wasted talent."

"What do you mean?" Jordyn asked.

"In addition to coaching me as a kid, Lenny used to coach Cadillac in a basketball youth league," Jasper answered.

Lenny stared at the TV. "He could'a been something. The next 'Zo or Shaq."

"Do you know where I might find him now? Or any of his friends?"

"If anyone knows where he is, it'd be George Butler. Runs a pool hall in South Florida. George and Cadillac were tight. He dated Cadillac's mom for a bit, so George was sort of a father figure to him for a while before things went south. I wouldn't count on him giving up Cadillac's location. Plus, he'll make you as a cop in seconds, assuming he doesn't remember you, in which case, he might be wondering why you ain't dead."

"I'll take my chances," Jasper said.

Thursday, August 29

Chapter 12 - Paul Dodd

PAUL SAT in the back of the transport van, alone, hands cuffed in front of him, on the way to another jail three counties away, thanks to his new attorney, Lawrence Kampf.

Though Paul was still in pain, his luck might be changing. The lawyer had somehow worked magic to get him out of Creek County.

"They never should've had you here," he'd said, arguing that there was no way Paul would be treated fairly once accused of killing a Creek County Deputy's child. Kampf promised to sue the hell out of the county and prove that they conspired to allow his rape.

When this is all said and done, not only will you be free, but you'll have a nice settlement and they will *pay.*

Paul smiled, thinking about the county being accountable for what they'd done.

It was funny. Even though Paul had committed these crimes — raped and murdered Ashley and tormented her mother — and maybe even deserved whatever hell might be coming his way, Kampf made him realize he was also a

victim. He had done some terrible things, yes, but that didn't abdicate the jail's obligation to keep him safe.

Nobody deserves what happened to you. Nobody.

Paul nearly broke down in tears, finally having someone on his side who wouldn't condemn him for his sickness. Someone who understood he couldn't help himself. Sure, the lawyer was being paid for his concern, but the only thing that mattered in the end was that he finally had a fighting chance.

Did he dare to imagine life outside of prison? Could he ever have a normal life again?

Even if he did get off, Paul would always be a suspect in the public's eyes. He was still dead to his wife and daughter. And the law would always be watching, waiting for him to slip up again.

Even if he was free, his life would never be the same. And he could never take another girl.

But that was fine.

He was ready to start over, to start fresh.

And he could probably find a way to satiate his needs without kidnapping and killing. Maybe he could move someplace where pimps trafficked children. He would have enough money to purchase a girl, take her from a life of slavery, offer her a room, hot meals, and showers. She might even be grateful enough to love him — something none of the other bitches had been capable of, spoiled as they were by western culture.

If Kampf managed to spring him and protect his assets, then Paul could do quite well in another country — a place where girls appreciated him.

A place where he wasn't seen as a monster because his tastes happened to run counter to "normal" people. A place where he could disappear. In a more permissive society, one where the law wasn't trying to crush him for his

predilections, perhaps he wouldn't feel the need to kill. Paul might find a girl he could come to love as she blossomed into a woman, free from the poison of feminism and western ideals.

He closed his eyes, imagining the girl. He wasn't particularly partial to Asians or dark-skinned girls in general, so maybe he could find a nice European, maybe from one of the former Russian countries. He imagined a beautiful blonde blue-eyed girl who'd been sold into slavery. Forced to endure the horrible men that came through, fucking and hurting her.

But Paul would be gentle and show her love.

The van made a series of odd choking sounds, then slowed before coming to a full stop.

The guards in the front were grumbling.

The door opened.

Footsteps, then the sound of a hood being raised, followed by a faint *POP, POP, POP!*

Then silence.

His nerves danced as he shifted in his seat.

Tires screeched to a stop behind the van.

More footsteps, moving fast.

What the hell is happening?

The rear doors opened, and bright light burned his eyes. Then it gave way to shapes, and Paul realized the men weren't guards. There were three, all armed and in masks, outfitted head to toe in black paramilitary gear.

The one in the middle was skinny, about Paul's height. But the other two were hulking steroid cases — like the Nazi who raped him.

No. No. No.

Are they part of his crew?

His heart froze, the taste of metal coating his tongue.

They've come to finish what they started!

Paul was helpless, cuffed to the van, unable to do anything but cry out for help.

Before he could get his mouth and brain to cooperate, the man in the middle said, "Make another sound and we kill you."

Paul obeyed the men as they boarded the van.

Chapter 13 - Jasper Parish

JASPER SAT in his rental car outside Corner Pocket, a dive bar-cum-pool hall located in the shittiest strip mall in the worst part of town. A rundown embarrassment of cinderblocks and concrete that hadn't seen a decent anchor chain since Zayre left in the eighties.

"This place looks sad," Jordyn said from the passenger seat, lifting the brim on her hat and training her phone's camera on a pigeon strutting around the cracked parking lot pavement.

"Used to be a nice plaza. Whole neighborhood used to be nice."

"What happened?"

"A sour economy, shady politicians and land developers, drugs, unemployment. People fled to the suburbs. Like dominos falling. The neighborhood never recovered."

In the twenty minutes they watched the place, only a few people had gone in. The windows were all painted black, so he couldn't see inside, but Jasper figured there were probably less than ten customers inside. The fewer people the better. Everyone knew everyone's business in

places like these, and it would be hard to get George to flip on Cadillac with regulars paying attention.

"Wait here. They might card you."

Jasper got out of his car, lowered his black Yankees cap over his eyes, and entered the Corner Pocket. The pool hall was large, but its better days were long behind it. Maybe it was some small mercy that the place was dark and poorly lit enough to hide its many flaws — stained threadbare carpet, chipped paint on the walls, tables starving for felt, sticks with broken tips. The only modern thing in the place was the hip-hop blasting from the jukebox.

Jasper was right. There were less than ten customers in the place — all but one, an old black man sitting at the end of the bar, were playing pool.

He scanned the place, but didn't see George, or any employee, so Jasper took a seat at the opposite end of the bar from the old man and waited.

After a few minutes, George came out of the back hefting a plastic tote full of ice. He deposited it into a cooler under the bar. He was one of those old guys who looked sixty at forty, then stayed that age for decades.

He looked up at Jasper and nodded. "What can I get for you, young man?"

"I'll have a Bud Light."

"Tap or bottle?"

"Bottle."

Jasper nursed his drink, occasionally glancing at the mirrored wall behind the bar, watching to see if anyone there might be affiliated with a gang or family. He wasn't getting even a whiff of organized crime, mostly just young people with nothing to do and older folks who'd given up on life, passing time by shooting pool. The old man at the end of the bar was either blitzed or out of his mind, maybe

both, mumbling to himself every now and then before finally laying his head on the bar.

Jasper could imagine a version of his life where he'd gone from troubled youth to aimless fool, wasting his days in places like this or running drugs, had Lenny not entered his life with the gifts of basketball and self-discipline.

George drifted over to him, wiping the bar with a rag. "Another Bud or will you be on your way?"

Jasper looked up and met the man's knowing eyes.

"I'm looking for Cadillac Taylor."

A flicker of recognition, then the old man turned his attention back to the rag. "Don't know him."

"I'm not police. Or an enemy."

"Yeah? Who are you then? Ain't ever seen you in these parts."

Jasper pulled out his phone, flashed a picture of Jessi Price. "You know her?"

"Nope." George gave a dismissive shrug, still pretending to wipe down the bar.

"A missing girl whose parents want her back. Cadillac can help me find her."

"How's that?"

"He helped kidnap the girl."

George's brow furrowed. He stopped wiping. "Man, get the hell out of here with your bullshit."

Jasper kept his voice low. "Listen, I'm not looking to jam him up. I'm guessing Cadillac got mixed up with some bad folks, but I don't care. I just want the girl back. They're willing to pay. So am I, if you help."

George paused, then went back to wiping the bar. "Get out of here. I ain't askin' twice."

Jasper grabbed the man's hand, hard, and locked gazes with him. "Here's the deal, George. I make one call, and

Curtis Johnson will send his boys over here to find out what you know. And they're definitely not offering you money."

He let go of the old man's hand and studied his face. Jasper had personalized the threat. Sometimes you had to add extra incentives, trying to win a person over with reason and promises that they were doing the right thing. But with someone like George, that would be seen as weakness. Far better to say less and let the threat hover above them, giving them enough time to appreciate the severity.

Jasper waited him out.

"I don't want your money," George finally said, practically spitting. The man was seconds from giving up Cadillac. "Stupid ass boy got himself a good job, but then found trouble, got fired, and I'm not sure what he's doing now. God only knows what he's into."

"Who was he working for?"

"You didn't get this from me."

Jasper nodded. "I just want to get that little girl back to her family."

"BlackBriar Security, a private firm. Good pay, dangerous work. Not sure how he screwed up. Just called me about four months ago saying he lost the job. But he refused to take any money, said he'd figure it out."

Jasper nodded. "Where is he now?"

"Last I heard he was staying in Jacksonville at The Carrington. Sounds like a nice place, but it's a shit hole in the projects."

"You did the right thing. Thank you."

"Hmm …" George grumbled, then went back to wiping the bar.

Jasper left the Corner Pocket, eager to leave a festering memory further behind.

Chapter 14 - Mallory Black

"HE'S ESCAPED," Mike said.

Mal didn't have to ask who. She moved the phone to her other ear. "How?"

"He was being transferred to another jail after his attack. The transport van was stopped and the guards shot dead. Now he's in the wind."

"Fuck!" Mal leaped out of bed and started pacing. She'd been awake for less than a minute.

"This seems highly organized. Did Dodd have connections to people with resources like——?"

"Not that I know of."

"One other thing. He's got a new lawyer, Lawrence Kampf, who petitioned for the transfer."

"Why the hell is *he* taking Dodd's case? Publicity?" Mal didn't wait before adding, "This can't be coincidence. You need to bring him in, see what he knows."

"We did. Or I should say, the Feds did. They're steering this bus. And, as you might expect, they got exactly shit from him."

"Fuck."

"I heard you reached out to Jessi's mom?"

"Yeah."

"You working another angle on this?"

"I'm just trying to help in any way I can." And then, after a long moment, she sighed, "Fuck. Poor Colleen. This public yet?"

"I'm sure it will be any minute."

"Double fuck. What about Dodd's ex-wife and their daughter, Lily? They in protective custody?"

"Arrangements are being made."

"Good. He warned me about this."

"Who?"

"Jasper Parish. He said this would happen, that Jessi would be taken again and that Paul would get out."

"How could he possibly know that?"

"You wouldn't believe me if I told you." She waited a beat. "He's psychic."

"What? You're not buying that bullshit, are you? They're working together, you ask me. And if that's the case, we need to get his info out there."

"I don't think so," Mal said. "I ... I believe him."

"Why? Doesn't it seem the least bit convenient that this dude knew about Ashley before she was taken and where to find you and Jessi when Paul took you back to your place? And he just happens to know about all this shit happening now? Come on, Mal. He's playing you. I don't know what his game is, but he's *not* psychic. There's no such thing."

It was funny between the two of them. Mike, the hard-core Catholic, was the skeptic. Maybe his religious background made it easy to dismiss the idea of psychic phenomena — one of those Christians that viewed anything they didn't understand as the work of the devil or con artists.

"He's not playing me. Don't ask me how I know, I just do. I can tell."

"Whatever. I just hope he does the right thing, whatever his game is."

"Me, too, partner. I'm going to call Colleen."

"Good luck. And hey, be careful. I can't help but think he might be coming back at you."

"Let him fucking try," Mal said, almost hoping he would. This time, she'd be well within her rights to kill the fucker dead.

She hung up and stared at the phone, trying to decide if she should call or warn Colleen in person. Her phone rang with a private number before she could decide. "Hello?"

"It's me," Jasper said.

"He's escaped."

"What? How?"

"Why don't you tell me, Mr. Psychic?"

"I don't know. But I warned you that he'd get out."

"He had help. Someone attacked the transport van."

"Lemme guess," Jasper said. "Same three men who attacked the bus?"

"I don't know yet."

"I might have something for you."

"What?"

"I wasn't going to pass this on. Because I wanted to investigate myself, but I'm out of town chasing leads." Jasper took a breath. "The man you're looking for is named Cadillac Taylor. Used to work for a mid-level drug dealer in South Florida named Lil' Tony. Boss got killed and Cadillac became a ghost. Went up to Jacksonville and started working with BlackBriar but lost that gig a few months ago. He's staying at The Carrington now."

"BlackBriar? As in the private security firm?"

"If you have contacts there, maybe they can help to point you toward his new employer."

"Thank you," Mal said, then added, "Can I ask you something?"

"Depends on the question."

"You're not working with Dodd, are you?"

"Really? You *still* don't trust me?"

"I don't trust anyone. And I'm not sure I'm buying the psychic-thing."

"Believe what you need to. But we're on the same side."

And with that, Jasper hung up.

Mal called Mike to tip him off about Cadillac, got his voice mail, and left a message with the details, except for the part about her source.

Then she paced some more, still feeling too deep on the sidelines. Mal didn't want to call Colleen without some plan of action or *something* she could do. She'd heard versions of "we've just gotta wait" plenty. More would only rot the poor woman's mind.

But Mal did know the CEO of BlackBriar, a man named Victor Forbes. She'd met him a few months ago at her home hotel. She was at the bar getting drunk, and he was in town for some event or another. He'd recognized her from the news and wanted to talk shop. In addition to hiring out private security to companies and military contractors, BlackBriar taught special courses to several law enforcement agencies in the South.

One thing led to another, and he plied her with expensive drinks before returning to his room.

In addition to being incredibly wealthy, Victor was young, good-looking, and full of himself. He came off like the prototypical Boy Scout in the press, but under the surface, he was anything but kind. He had a dark streak,

the kind that served as a magnet for self-destructive people. Exactly the sort of man Mal was attracted to at her worst.

They had a good time, from what she could remember. She even fell asleep in his bed, something she normally never did with one-night-stands.

He gave her his number and said he'd love to "do this again."

She never called, but she still had his number in her phone — assuming it wasn't a fake.

Mal looked it up and dialed. After a few rings he answered.

"Hello?"

"It's Mallory Black. Remember me?"

A moment's pause, then, "Yes. Yes I do. I thought maybe you'd lost my number."

She laughed coyly. Guys like this needed it cool. "Was busy with work, you know. But I took some time off, and I'm in your neck of the woods for a few days. Got time to grab a late lunch?"

It was a long shot, Victor's calendar was probably full. But he also seemed like the sort of guy that liked to break away, tell his assistant to hold everything while he dropped out of pocket and *indulged*.

She waited through the silence until he said, "Where are you staying?"

She picked the nicest hotel she knew of, Twenty-One Resort & Spa on the beach.

"I'll see if I can clear things up. This a good number to reach you at?"

"Yes."

"I'll be in touch." And then Victor hung up.

Mal felt guilty using false pretenses to arrange a meeting, but he was the sort of guy who would never met a cop for questioning without a lawyer. His company had a few

rotten apples do some bad shit in the Middle East a few years back, and it took years to wash that stink away. If the FBI started sniffing around Cadillac Taylor, and they eventually would, Victor would likely go underground until he and his team crafted a response that would portray Black-Briar in the best possible light.

No, we don't hire criminals as a matter of course. No, we don't know why he would kidnap Jessi Price or break Paul Dodd out of jail. No, our company doesn't endorse any of these actions.

Mal's way was faster. Assuming the Feds didn't make the connection first.

Chapter 15 - Mallory Black

MAL SAT in the restaurant on the bottom floor of Twenty-One Resort & Spa, scrolling through her phone in search of any breaking news on Jessi as she waited for Victor to show. Finding nothing, she checked her messages, hoping for something from Mike.

Nothing new yet.

She had called Colleen on her way to the resort, breaking the news of Dodd's escape. She hated doing it over the phone, knowing the woman would need someone to console her, but Mal comforted Colleen by explaining that she was working on a lead and wouldn't rest until they got Jessi back and threw Dodd behind bars.

She was about to text Mike to see if they'd acted on her tip yet when she looked up and saw Victor making his way to her table, dapper in his charcoal suit and an ice-blue tie. It matched his eyes exactly. His blond hair was slicked back into a ponytail. The light stubble looked rebellious, even though the rest of him was GQ CEO.

He smiled as he approached. She stood, and he hugged her. "Good to see you again, Mallory."

They took their seats. The waitress appeared like a magic trick, asking what they'd like to drink.

"We'll have two glasses of the Adler Deutsch Reserve Cabernet," he said, then turned to Mal. "Will that work for you."

Mal nodded. Indeed, it would.

As the waitress went to fetch their drinks, Victor ignored his menu and looked at her, his eyes and smile both surprisingly warm.

Mal felt bad for lying to get him here. This was the kind of thing she could do exactly once before turning a person off and having them never answer her call again. Victor was a good person to know, someone with information and resources. Someone who could help.

And she was about to screw things up.

The waitress brought their wine and asked if they wanted to order. Victor said to swing back by in a bit, they were catching up.

She smiled then left.

Victor raised his glass. "To your health."

They clinked glasses and Mal sipped, wishing for something less fragrant and a lot harder.

"So, what brings you round here?"

"Well, I wish I could say it was pleasure. But I'm actually following a lead."

Victor's mouth turned ever-so-slightly downward. He set his glass on the table and adjusted his smile to mask the disappointment.

"Ah, okay. How can I help you?" His face was friendly, but she could see him erecting walls in his head, bracing for something.

"I didn't mean to trick you into coming here, but this is a life-and-death matter for a little girl who could die if I don't find the man I'm looking for."

He seemed to relax, a bit. "Who are you looking for?"

"A former employee of yours, Cadillac Taylor. We believe he may have helped to kidnap Jessi Price." She left out the part about Dodd, for now.

"What?" Victor seemed genuinely surprised. "Cadillac Taylor kidnapped that missing girl?"

"We're looking into it. Someone told me he was let go from BlackBriar. Can you tell me anything about why he was let go and where we might find him?"

"As to where he is, I'd have to call HR. As for why we let him go, without going into minutia, he wasn't a fit for BlackBriar. Showed up late a few times, then failed a drug test."

"What did he do?"

"Private detail for a few clients."

"Any chance we could get a list of those clients?"

"You know we can't do that, not without a court order. Discretion is part of the job."

"I'm just trying to get a jump on this before the Feds come. I'm not saying this as a threat, Victor. I'm off duty now, helping the girl's mother. I think you can respect me not wanting to sit and wait through all the red tape. I want to get this girl home. I was with her the first time Dodd took her. And now he's out of jail, too. I can only imagine the hell he has planned for her. *Please*, Victor, I'll settle for whatever you can give me."

She put her hand in his, knowing he probably saw through the move but hoping her last play might work anyway.

"Okay, I'm giving this to you, not the Feds. Okay?"

"Yes."

"He was friends with this other guy who worked for us, a real bastard named Christopher Stanwicz — beat his girlfriend and was stalking her, had some ugly issues with

women. Not sure how he passed our background check and psych tests, but after an arrest for terrorizing his ex, we let him go. He bonded out then disappeared. We learned later that he used to work with some shady people in organized crime. Maybe he went back, got a job, then needed another disgruntled worker to help him? It's not much, but that's all I've got."

"Thank you," Mal said.

"Still in the mood for lunch?"

"You're not mad at me?"

"Well, I am curious why you didn't just ask me over the phone."

"Would you believe me if I said I wanted to see you?"

He smiled. "No, not really."

"I don't like doing things over the phone, not when it comes to a case like this."

"Well, perhaps I should let you get back to work?"

"Raincheck on the lunch?"

"I'm holding you to it," he said.

"After the case is over, I'll make it up to you. Thanks for understanding."

Mal reached into her wallet to drop some cash for the wine, but Victor raised a hand to stop her.

She hugged him goodbye, then headed to her car with a name — *Christopher Stanwicz.*

She called Mike. This time he answered.

"Did you get the info I sent?"

"Yeah, we went to Cadillac's place, but the dude's in the wind. The Feds grabbed a laptop, so maybe they'll find something, but I'm not holding out any hope."

"Any word on Jessi or Paul?"

"Nothing more," Mike said.

Mal told him about her conversation with Victor, then gave him the new name.

Mike laughed.

"What?"

"It's bullshit that you're not working this case. Hell, you're the only one getting anything useful."

"Well, Bell has to protect her image. It's all about November."

"You know this is eating her up, right? Gloria would love to have you on this, almost as much as I would. You know this is how it had to go down."

Mal hated that her past couple of years of misery were being used against her. Hated that the media was more concerned about her drinking and beating up a couple of assholes who deserved it than the former sheriff's blatant disregard of civil rights or the allegations of corruption surrounding his administration.

Gloria Bell had made the sheriff's office respectable again, not an easy thing to do when a good chunk of the county hated the woman for either her color or political affiliation. And now, because Barry and his cohorts couldn't win in a clean election by debating the facts, they were looking to take the sheriff down by using Mal, regardless of any real world consequences.

"Yeah, well, I fucked up. I just hope that Jessi doesn't have to pay for my sins."

Chapter 16 - Mallory Black

MAL STOOD OUTSIDE HER HOUSE, cool wind blowing and storm clouds blotting out the afternoon sun, keys clutched tight in her hand as she stared at the front door.

She wasn't sure how she ended up here. She'd been driving back from her meeting with Victor when she began to mourn the loss of her home. It was a shame, living in a hotel like she was. Returning to the house had been hard after Dodd brought her and Jessi there to rape and murder them both.

While Mal enjoyed hotel amenities like the cleaning staff, the concierge who always had whatever toiletry she'd neglected to buy, and the downstairs restaurant and bar, this was the house where she, Ray, and Ashley had made a home for so long.

But with her ex-husband having moved on and their daughter dead, the house was a graveyard, host to painful memories and a reminder of what could never be again.

Yet, she couldn't sell it.

Because some of those memories were good. And every time she went into Ashley's room, Mal still felt her

presence, in her toys, clothes, and favorite stuffed animals. Lying in her old bed, Mal could close her eyes and remember what she might have otherwise forgotten — reading at night, hiding under the covers and waiting for The Daddy Monster to tickle them, and simple moments like when Ashley would stare at Mal with her big blue eyes and say, "I love you, Mommy" for no reason other than to hear her own whisper.

Selling the house would mean closing the door on those memories.

Then, as she stood on the front porch about to insert her key, the tainted images came. She heard Jessi's cries, saw the look of fear her eyes as Paul straddled her with Mal helplessly cuffed to the bed.

Dodd had taken the sanctity of her home, of Ashley's room, and ruined them.

Mal wasn't sure what she'd feel going into that bedroom again. Would she see her daughter, or Jessi writhing in pain, anticipating the horror of her approaching rape and murder?

"Fuck this," Mal whispered to herself.

She unlocked the front door, marched through the living room then up the stairs, eager to banish those terrible memories for good. Reclaim Ashley's room for herself and her daughter.

She reached Ashley's door, reached for the knob, and froze.

Then she collapsed to the hallway floor, sobbing.

Dodd was in her head, and the monster refused to leave.

Mal had seen many dark things in her years as a detective, the sort of stuff she didn't used to think humans were capable of, the things she usually had to bury deep or find herself unable to go on.

None of that came close to the darkness that swallowed her after losing Ashely, or the hate that boiled for the man responsible.

Sitting outside Ashley's room, Mal flashed back to the climax of so many nightmares — when she had a chance to put him down. Jasper offered her the gift of killing Dodd, to get vengeance for Ashley, Jessi, and God only knew how many other girls.

Mall could have ended him there. But she couldn't kill a man in cold blood, even a monster like Dodd. But Jasper's offer rang again in her head, taunting her. Had she listened the first time, Jessi would probably be safe at home.

Mal screamed and punched. She clawed at the carpet.

And then she was up, walking to her room, to the nightstand, to her bottle of pills.

She unscrewed the cap and looked inside. Three left.

No. You've been so good. Do not take them. Don't —

Her phone rang. Mike.

She picked it up, sat on her bed, thankful to hear a friendly voice. She wanted to tell him where she was, that she was considering taking pills.

But he spoke before she could. "We checked on that name you gave us, Christopher Stanwicz."

"And?"

"Found him in his kitchen, gunshot to the head, suicide note to his ex, saying sorry but he couldn't live without her."

"What the fuck? How long ago did he die?"

"A couple of days old, judging from the corpse."

"Fuck. Any *good* news?"

"Nothing. How about you? Jasper give you anything else?"

"No," Mal said, slipping into a hopeless void. "We need to find her, Mike—"

"We will."

Mike rarely made such promises. He knew, same as she did, that as each hour faded, so did the odds of finding Jessi alive. Maybe he could sense her desperation.

A long silence yawned between them. Mal wondered if he knew what she was about to do. Was he trying to decide how best to intervene? Should he be the stern but loving friend or commiserate with a shoulder to cry on?

Mal hated needing anybody, even more imposing on someone, especially her work partner.

She opened her mouth, about to tell him she needed him to come over, to help her get through this, but then she heard a clicking followed by a pause. "Gloria's calling. You okay?"

"Yeah, yeah, I'm good. Talk to you later."

Mal hung up, stared at the phone, then thumbed through her contacts. Ray was the only person who might understand what she was going through, but now he was gone.

So fuck him.

Mal went up and down the list, her sorrow settling as she saw person after person who had either been a friend she'd lost touch with or strangers who might have been something more had she ever invested the time.

Her contact list was a front-page reminder of her worth as a human.

Mal froze on Tim Brentwood, one person she hadn't burned or ignored. He worked Narcotics in Jacksonville. A one-night-stand who also showed some promise. But she couldn't call him now, not when she felt this weak.

Hey, Tim, remember me? Yeah, I'm feeling about as low as you

can fucking feel, and I'm really wanting to do some pills, so how about we hook up and you can take my mind off my miserable life?

She grabbed the bottle and shook it.

Three pills.

Just three.

Three pills never killed anyone, did they?

Mal raised them to her mouth, popped them in, and just as she was about to swallow, an ugly history rumbled through her mouth. She thought of her daughter, and the deep disappointment that would surely mar her face, if only she could see it.

She spit out the pills, then went downstairs to the fridge and found a bottle of beer. Mal unscrewed the cap and swallowed, taking the bottle back to her room.

She fell back on the bed, hoping the booze would serve as a salve to her agony.

Chapter 17 - Mallory Black

MAL WOKE UP NAUSEOUS, just after seven. She made her way to the bathroom and puked, then took a shower to wake herself and freshen up.

She considered going to a Narcotics Anonymous meeting, to help her fight the urge to use, but the last thing she needed now was some asshole in there shooting video and selling it to some other dickhead in the media. Then she'd never get her job back.

An awful thought occurred to her. She might have to take a drug test once she returned to work. She couldn't do pills even if she wanted to. And that, of course, made her crave them even more.

Fuck!

She got dressed, went out to her car, and started driving, looking for something to move her mind away from the pain.

She wound up at Grommet's Pub, a trendy sports bar on the beach, took a booth in the back, then ordered a burger, fries, and beer.

She sipped the ice-cold draft, waiting for her food and

scoping the place out. It was busy for a Thursday night in August, when most area businesses were still waiting for the snowbirds to come down and pack their places. The crowd skewed older, transplants from New York or California, and too many people who looked like they'd be right at home on the lawn at a Jimmy Buffet show, most of them sitting at the bar watching a game and getting drunk. A few couples and groups were eating dinner in booths, including a few familiar faces, but no one noticed Mal in her cap and ponytail.

The waitress, an older blonde with sun-speckled skin, brought her food then asked Mal if she wanted anything else. She raised her empty mug. "A few more of these."

Mal ate the burger and drank more beer, checking the local news sites. If there had been any updates, Mike would've called. But with the Feds in charge, it was impossible to know if something might leak before he had a chance to tell her.

Mal tapped the Kindle app and started reading a book on grief that she'd bought a few months ago. She read, then drank, and ordered a shot of Jack when the beer kept refusing to buzz.

She looked up and spotted the fucker who had made her life miserable ever since appearing on her radar promising to fuck with the sheriff's department: *Cameron Ford.*

He was sitting at the other end of the restaurant with an older man in a beige bucket hat and a flannel shirt. Merle Truman, the man who ran Truman's Fishing and Hunting Superstore. He *just so happened* to be a close friend of Claude Barry. One of the original good ol' boys, Merle's family had lived in Creek County forever, pulling the strings of county commissioners for just as long.

His power, same as most of the influential west siders,

slipped the moment Pine Harbour incorporated in the seventies. The west side was full of white farmers whose families had been here forever. Pine Harbour was a fresh city filled with New Yorkers, South Floridians, and a host of non-natives whom the west-siders resented for innumerable reasons.

Many west-siders figured that when the next building boom came, they were sitting on prime real estate that would attract factories and retail, but when they couldn't get their land use changed from agricultural to something better, they lost millions and needed someone to blame. Some of that boiled over into violence against city folks, sometimes with a racist edge.

Sheriff Barry, a longtime west-sider, ignored much of it during his watch.

Seeing Cameron hanging around with Barry's proxy was all the confirmation Mal needed to connect the dots she'd been seeing for a while.

Mal raised her phone and snapped some photos of them chatting as they ate. Anger brewed as she considered the damage that Cameron had done with his blog posing as legitimate news.

He'd been responsible for a lynch mob by casting blame on a mentally challenged man in the death of a little girl. Then he got Mal put on leave, unable to work. All in the last month.

And now he was laughing through dinner.

The waitress set her shot on the table. Mal thanked her and swallowed.

She stood, dropped two twenties on the table, grabbed her purse and phone, then went over to Cameron.

He looked up, his eyes wide.

Mal grabbed a nearby chair, set it at the end of their booth, flipped it backwards, dropped her purse between

her legs and the chair's back, and straddled the seat. She rested her elbows on the table and smiled. "Hey, guys. How's it going?"

They traded confused glances before Merle faked a smile. "Well, hello, Detective, how are you tonight?"

"Oh, I'm spiffy. And you two?" She ignored Merle, fixing her gaze on Cameron, eyeing her nervously. "You all seen the news? Jessi Price being taken again? And Paul Dodd escaping?"

"Yeah, that's a damned shame," Merle said.

"And thanks to your boy, here," she pointed at Cameron, "I can't work the case."

Cameron cleared his throat. "Hey, don't put your drunken behavior on me. I'm only doing my job. It's a little thing called integrity, you might try it some time."

Mal laughed. "With a hit piece designed to make the sheriff's office look bad? Yeah, that doesn't have anything at all to do with your puppet master, does it?"

Merle's smile faded and his hard blue eyes settled on her. "Listen here, young lady. Your boss did a fair enough job disgracing her office. But you go on ahead and blame everyone but her and yourself. You Libs are great at that."

Mal was squarely in the middle on most things and not about to let this fucker alter her argument.

She smiled at Merle. "See, the only thing I'm having trouble figuring out is whose hand is up whose ass? Is Berry's up yours, or is your hand up his? Everyone is up poor Cameron's, isn't that right? How does that feel, having Conlan's pedo hands all up in there, and now these two? All that *integrity* up in your ass like a fist. You like that Mr. Ford?"

Cameron's face was already bright red, his eyes boring into hers.

She hoped he'd take a swing but doubted he would. He

was a big talker on his website or behind a mic but a fucking coward when confronted.

Merle said, "I see you've learned your lesson, of getting drunk in public and assaulting people."

"I haven't assaulted anyone, *yet*." She fixed her gaze on him, hoping like hell he'd make a grab for the knife in his pocket or something.

Cameron had his camera on her. "We're asking you politely to stop threatening us, Detective Mallory Black. Do we need to call the sheriff's office?"

She wanted to wipe the smile from his smarmy face. But his camera was cold water on her boiling rage. She wanted to grab his phone, throw it to the ground, and crush it under her heel, but that would end her career, and the fucking blogger would probably earn her lottery winnings for the trouble.

"Give my best to your friend, Sheriff Barry." Mal smiled, stood, then grabbed her bag and phone.

She went out to her car, got inside, and punched the steering wheel as she screamed.

Then she realized she wasn't alone.

Mal looked in the rearview just as the man in shadows leaned forward and pressed his gun to the back of her head.

Chapter 18 - Jasper Parish

"HANDS ON THE WHEEL, THEN FREEZE," Jasper said.

She stared at him through tears, her hands gripping the wheel. "What do *you* want?"

"Checking in to see if your partner got anything on Cadillac."

"Can you put the fucking gun down? I'm having a shit night and don't need you accidentally shooting me."

She was wasted, the stench of alcohol heavy in the car, her speech slurred.

"Fair enough," Jasper lowered the gun. "What did you get?"

"He worked for BlackBriar for a while, but they let him go. The CEO said Cadillac might be working with a guy named Christopher Stanwicz. He ran with a sketchy crowd. Problem is, when we went to go check on the guy, he'd been dead for a few days already."

"They're cleaning their tracks. Who is the CEO? How do you know him?"

"Victor Forbes. I met him a couple years back."

"Do you trust him?"

"More than I trust men sneaking into my car in the middle of the night."

Jasper smiled. Mallory reminded him a bit of his daughter.

"Something else that might be of interest to you," she said. "The day before Dodd was transferred out, he was sexually assaulted in prison. Anyway, the very next day, a high-profile lawyer swoops in, takes his case, and gets him transferred. Then, poof, Dodd is sprung by some mystery men."

"Did your partner or the Feds talk to the lawyer?"

"Yes, but they got nothing from him. This dude is good."

"What's his name?"

"Why? You going to pay him a visit?"

"The less you know the better."

"I don't want him showing up dead."

"You brought him up for a reason, right? You want me to find out what you couldn't?"

"Well, conventional methods aren't working right now. And," Mallory started crying again, "I just want Jessi back home with her mom."

That wasn't *all* she wanted, of course. She also wanted Dodd behind bars, or maybe she'd even come around to wanting him dead. But he didn't press it. She was in tears, and few things made him feel more helpless than a woman crying.

"We're going to find her," Jasper said.

"Says the psychic."

"Ye of little faith." He opened the door and started to get out of the car. But then he held out his hand instead. "Give me your keys."

"What?"

"You're drunk. The last thing you need is a DUI."

"So, what, you're going to take me home?"

"Why not?"

She shook her head and handed him her keys. "Fine."

He came around to the driver's side and opened the door, allowing Mallory to get out.

She froze in front of him, looking him up and down as if thinking maybe she might apprehend her suspect after all.

Jasper considered warning her, maybe even showing her his gun again, but then she pushed past him, walked around the front of the car, got in like a petulant teenager, then slammed the door.

"Where am I going? Your hotel or your house?"

"You been following me?"

He smiled. "You said you're having a bad night. What happened?"

Her arms were crossed. She stared out the window, again reminding him of Jordyn.

"It doesn't matter."

"Man, you're a moody ass drunk."

She glared at him.

He smiled wider. "I'm just busting your balls. Seriously, though, what happened?"

She told him about her run-in with "that asshole, Cameron Ford and his fucking puppeteer, Merle Truman," and how Cameron's had a hard-on for her ever since he worked at *The Chronicle*, where her ex was a photographer. He published photos of Ashley's corpse on his personal Twitter account and she, or rather Ray, got him fired.

"He vanished for a while, was working at some rag in Wisconsin. Then he showed up six months ago, just as things were leading up to the election. The fucker was working with Conlan and Barry. They're trying to make

Bell look bad by making *me* look unstable and getting me put on leave so I can't do a damned thing to help Jessi."

"You want me to take care of him?"

"I'd love that," Mallory said, before quickly taking it back, waving her hands to amplify her response. "No, no I *do not* want you to 'take care' of him. I don't want you 'taking care' of anyone! Do you understand me?"

"I was kidding." Then Jasper smiled again. "Well, sorta."

Mallory snickered. "What's your deal? Why are you doing all of this?"

"I'm tired of seeing the bad guys win."

"So, you're the judge and jury now?"

"I am."

"That's bullshit."

"How?"

"You don't get to choose who is innocent and guilty. That's what the legal system is for." A beat, then, "What if you're wrong?"

Jasper glanced at the empty road, then met her eyes. "I'm never wrong."

"Hmmph."

"I don't go around randomly killing people. I only target genuine threats. If I knew who Paul Dodd was before he murdered Ashley, I would have killed him."

"Don't bring my daughter into this. She's not some justification for your sickness."

"I'm not sick."

"Whatever," Mallory said, her gaze back out the window.

"If you knew without a doubt someone was going to kill a child and had done so before, knew his death was the only way you could really stop him, would you do it?"

"You can't know."

"But if you did?"

"I'm not playing this game."

"Wanna know what I think?"

"I'm sure you're going to tell me."

"I think you damned well would do whatever you could to save an innocent child. Including kill."

"I'm an officer, sworn to uphold the law, not take it into my own hands. Enforcing your version of the law undermines the justice system. If everyone did that, we'd have chaos. The law is there to keep civilization from descending into a might-equals-right, dog-eat-dog mess."

Jasper nodded. "I can respect that, Detective. For other people. But not me. I'm right. *Always*."

"Lawrence Kampf," Mallory said after a moment of silence. "That's Dodd's new lawyer. But you'd better not harm him."

"Thank you."

Jasper pulled into her driveway, stopped the car and handed Mallory the keys. "It was nice chatting with you."

"How are you going to get back to ... well, wherever it is you're going?"

"I'll get a ride. Go get some sleep. And ... be careful."

Jasper closed the door and ran away from her house, into the darkness. He had another visit to make. Though he had absolutely no intention of honoring his passenger's request.

One way or another, the lawyer would talk.

Chapter 19 - Paul Dodd

PAUL WOKE UP, looked around at what appeared to an opulent hotel suite, and wondered if he was dreaming. The sunken living room was large, almost obscenely so, and the fixtures — though clearly uniform — were dark and polished and new.

His prison jumpsuit had been replaced with blue silk pajamas.

The last thing he remembered was following a man out of the van. Everything went black after that. Had he been drugged? Knocked out? Paul wasn't sure, but he sat up feeling dizzy and had to wait a moment before daring to stand.

Where the hell am I?

Who are these people?

Why would they take me?

He waited, the irony of his abduction not lost, until the door finally opened. He flinched, half expecting some maniac to charge him with a machete. Instead, Paul was greeted by a thin, dark-skinned young man dressed in a

fine white suit. He looked like he had escaped a Calvin Klein ad.

"Hello, Mr. Dodd." His accent was thick, Spanish perhaps. He stood at the doorway, holding a tray with a covered plate and a glass of ice water. "Your dinner is served."

Paul who made space on the bed for the tray. It was silver with looping ivy engraved around the perimeter. He was suspicious, but the smell of meat and whatever else was under the covered plate set his stomach to grumbling.

"Where am I?"

"You're in Paraíso. My name is Daniel, and I'll be taking care of you this evening. Anything you need, don't hesitate to dial."

He eyed the phone on the nightstand and wondered if he could use it to call out. But who would care that he'd been taken? Paul was an escaped prisoner, and this place was obviously better than whatever jail he was on his way to.

Daniel lifted the cover.

It had been so long since Paul had eaten anything other than the prison pablum. The sight of a perfectly seared filet, dollop of garlic mash, and what looked like lightly battered and fried asparagus overrode any trepidation he had over who had accosted him.

He unwrapped his fork and knife from the cloth napkin then shoveled food into his mouth like a shipwreck survivor.

The food was heavenly, worth five and a half stars. It obviously wasn't cheap. If someone had kidnapped Paul, he was curious as to who they were and why the hell they had gone to so much trouble.

It had to be the lawyer. Wes's money. Somehow this was all tied to him.

But how?

"What is Paraíso?" Paul asked through a mouthful of steak. "A resort, or what?"

"It's a discreet destination for men with particular tastes, tailored to their needs." And then Daniel left, heading back outside to a cart in the hallway before returning with a bottle of wine and a glass.

"Château Haut-Bailly Pessac-Léognan. If this is not to your liking, we have an extensive collection to choose from." Daniel uncorked the bottle and poured wine into a goblet.

"This'll be fine." Paul took a sip. He wasn't much of a wine guy, but it went down easily. "So, Daniel, why am I here … in Paraíso?"

"After you're finished with your meal, you can use the shower to freshen up. You'll find a change of clothing in the closet. Get dressed, ring me, and I'll bring you to Madam. She will answer your questions."

"Okay." Because what else could he say?

"Will there be anything else?"

"No. Thank you."

Daniel left, closing the door softly behind him and locking it.

Even in Paraíso, Paul was no less a prisoner.

He finished his meal, the wine, and the glass of water. No longer dizzy, he went to the bathroom. It had a whirlpool tub and a separate shower, with a handful of shower heads and an orgy's worth of room.

It had been forever since he'd had a nice, warm bath, so Paul filled the tub, and even added some bubbles. He undressed, slid into the almost-scalding water, and closed his eyes, allowing himself to shut out the rest of the world and its problems, even if only for a while.

He wasn't sure what the rest of the resort was like, but the tub delivered on its promise.

After his relaxing bath, Paul found clothes in the closet. He had several pairs of pants and shirts to choose from, all in his size. He got dressed, called Daniel, then found the man standing at the door three minutes later.

"Are you ready to meet her?"

"Yes."

Daniel led him out of his room and into a long hall with rich crimson carpet, loud art hanging on softly colored walls or painted directly on them, including a stunning display of *trompe l'œil*.

Paul counted four doors on either side of the hallway on their way to the elevator. "These other rooms, are they also prisoners?"

"You're not a prisoner. But to answer your question, this is our most private wing, for guests such as yourself whom require extra discretion.

Paul heard the giggling of young-sounding women as they passed one of the rooms. He wanted to stop and eavesdrop at the door but resisted the urge.

They reached the elevator. Daniel slid a card over a scanner, then it slid open.

It was spacious inside, mirrored. A camera looked down from the corner.

Paul's eyes fell to the floor.

The elevator dinged open to a dark club with thumping electronica, colorful lights flickering to the beat, and a DJ high in the center of it all, looking like something out of mid-90s MTV.

Paul followed Daniel, his vision bewildered by the staccato bursts of light. It was sensory overload, people dancing in the strobing dark, half-naked women and men

gyrating on the dance floor, people making out in booths that would've put any strip club's VIP room to shame.

A topless waitress in a glowing blue-and-pink necklace with teeth that shined white in the black light, approached Paul with a tray of vials of red and yellow drinks.

"Shot?" she asked in a Russian accent.

He considered it but didn't want his senses dulled while meeting Madam. "No, thank you." Paul pushed his way past her, but not before getting one last look at her perfectly perky breasts. Then he lost Daniel. Stopping to look for his guide, Paul saw something that set his heart to pounding — an old Asian man sitting in a booth with two pre-pubescent girls in tiny bikinis and plenty of makeup.

One of the girls was giggling, snorting cocaine off the table. The other girl climbed onto his lap.

This place is Paradise!

Daniel found him, though Paul no longer wanted to follow him. Not when he could sit and watch, maybe even join the party.

He stared at the girls, aroused. The girl on the old man's lap looked up at Paul and smiled coyly. Then she closed her eyes, moaning as the man reached under the table and into her lap.

The girl doing coke started to kiss the other girl, letting her hand trail down.

Where the hell did they find young girls so sexual?

Though Paul was partial to the innocence of girls and hated when they turned into bitches and sluts, he'd never seen anything like this — children so into sex. And unlike most of the child porn he'd seen, these girls didn't look dead inside or have that glassy-eyed expression. They were into it and happy.

Daniel said, "Ah, I see you've found something that piques your interest?"

"You could say that."

"We can have a video catalog sent to your room after you meet with Madam. While I believe these particular ladies are busy for the next few days, we have several others to choose from. And if we don't have what you like, we can get it."

"*Several* others? How?"

"As I said, Mr. Dodd, in Paraíso, we exist to please."

Paul managed to break his attention from the girls and the old man then follow Daniel, his eyes scanning every pocket of darkness for more salacious activities. He found plenty of making out and even some fucking, though mostly by adults, or close enough. He spotted one other child, but this time it was a boy and two men on either side of him, watching the kid eat ice cream. One of them was jerking off as the boy ate, which disturbed Paul, mostly because he didn't like boys. In fact, he felt a pang of sympathy for the child, hoping he wouldn't have to endure anything too rough.

At a stairwell, they descended to a red door. Two large armed men with severe crew cuts stood outside. The one on the right looked Paul up and down, then nodded them through.

Daniel opened the door, then Paul walked through to meet the woman with answers.

"Hello, Mr. Dodd. I am Madam Pandora." She was a short, thin Spanish woman in a red silk dress. Long jet-black hair hung straight, covering the left side of her face almost entirely. She looked to be in her early forties but could have been a decade younger or older. It was hard to tell in such low light and with half her face buried. In either case, she was classically beautiful, and her smile was warm. But her eyes were cold and dilated with secrets.

She sat behind a desk flanked by two faux red trees in

this small, dark, room. The walls were black, their dark expanse broken by two doors. Paul could practically feel armed men behind them, waiting for the word to strike.

"Please, have a seat." She waved a hand at the chair in front of her desk, her voice demure.

Paul sat and Daniel left, closing the door behind him.

Madam Pandora sat across from him, bolt upright, hands folded on the desk. She was either the most poised person he'd ever met or an obsessive control freak.

"Welcome to Paraíso. I'm assuming you have questions."

"Um, yeah. Where am I? Why am I here? And what *is* this place?"

"All excellent questions. You are in Paraíso, a resort for a very select clientele. We're in El Barranco, in Mexico, where you can hide from your government. And you are here because you have something we want."

"What's that?"

"Your benefactor, Mr. Wes Richardson, was one of the founding members of our little group. He was also a slightly paranoid man, and being such, he kept a flash drive in a safe deposit box at Banco Montaña BPI. Now that he's passed, we'd hate for that information to fall into the wrong hands."

"What does that have to do with me?"

"I'm guessing Mr. Richardson thought very highly of you, seeing as he left you that box. We'd like you to recover that flash drive and bring it to us."

Paul wanted to know what was on the drive, but he'd already seen enough to know better than to ask a question which might put his life in danger. These were powerful people with a criminal empire to uphold. No reason to piss them off with an idiot's questions.

"And how do I do that? Just walk in the bank and get it? I'm a fugitive."

"That's in the States, Mr. Dodd. So long as we act quickly, I don't anticipate any issues. Mr. Richardson left you a key. They're going to want to match your thumbprint to what they have on file."

"And how do they have my thumbprint on file?"

"You'd have to ask Mr. Richardson."

"After I give you this flash drive, what then? Are you sending me back?"

"Oh, heavens no," Madam said with a polite laugh. "After that, you are free to live out your days wherever you want. We would be eternally grateful if you could do us this one favor, enough that we've procured your first gift in advance."

"What's that?" Paul shifted in his seat, thinking of the Nazi, imagining one of the doors opening to some thug who might come to beat him into compliance.

Instead, Madam Pandora reached into her desk, pulled out an iPad, and slid her fingers across the glass surface, navigating a screen that Paul couldn't see. Then she handed him the tablet.

"I trust you're pleased?"

He looked down at the screen and saw the impossible — Jessi Price in a room like his.

"She's here, Mr. Dodd. Our gift to you."

Friday, August 30

Chapter 20 - Jasper Parish

JASPER SAT in front of a convenience store drinking a Coke in his rental while surveying Kampf's two-story beachfront home across the road and just down the street, waiting to see if anyone would leave.

"Maybe his wife isn't home," Jordyn suggested from the passenger seat.

"Maybe, but I'm not taking chances. I'd prefer not to hurt any innocents."

"So, what do we do, just sit here all day?"

"It's not even seven in the morning. Chill."

"I'm bored." She sighed.

He laughed. "You would make a terrible cop."

"What's the longest stakeout you ever had to stay on?"

"Once we got a tip that this dealer was holed up in this apartment, but we couldn't grab him until he left."

"Why?"

"We didn't want to arrest him. We wanted to flip him to get to his boss. So we sat there for almost fourteen hours, and he didn't so much as open a curtain, let alone leave."

"What did you do in situations like that, like if you had to pee or … worse?"

Jasper shook his fountain drink.

"Oh, that is soooo gross. You did that with your partner in the car?"

"When you've gotta go, you've gotta go."

Jordyn wrinkled her face in disgust, then her eyes widened. "I've got an idea! I'm gonna look on her LiveLyfe page. See if she mentioned any plans for the day."

"Good idea. See, you're not completely useless."

Jordyn rolled her eyes, then flipped down the screen, saw something of interest, and handed her phone to Jasper. He saw a photo of Lawrence's wife, Kathleen, posing with drinks, sitting beside another woman in a restaurant. She pointed. "See the location?"

"New York."

"Yep," Jordyn said. "She's out of town."

"Then I'm going in. You're waiting down the street."

"Oh, come on. Can't I come this time?"

"No, and don't ask again."

Jordyn sighed as Jasper drove to a spot a few houses down. He jogged along the beach behind the lawyer's neighbors, then looked both ways to see if anyone was paying attention before pulling a mask over his face and vaulting the white fence.

He was in the backyard with a fenced-in patio and well-maintained plants and shrubs. The home's entire rear was windowed, none of the curtains or shades drawn. If Lawrence happened to look out, he'd spot Jasper immediately.

He hoped the fat fucker was still in bed.

The patio door was unlocked. Jasper let himself inside, hoping his luck wouldn't fade.

The first of two sliding glass doors, one looking into the

living room, was locked. He went to the one off the kitchen — Lawrence was sitting at the bar eating breakfast while watching TV.

Jasper ducked, hoping the guy didn't spot him. The last thing he wanted to do was give the guy time to find his gun, assuming he had one. A safe assumption, given his station.

He didn't wait long to peek again. The man was gone from his spot.

Shit!

He tried the sliding glass door, relieved when he found it unlocked.

Jasper slid it slowly on the track. The heavy door moved silently enough. He entered the dining area and saw that the lawyer's plate was still half-filled with eggs and bacon, his orange juice still three quarters full.

Had Lawrence gone to the bathroom or to get his gun?

Jasper retrieved his blade and moved fast through the bottom floor until he found himself at the foot of the stairs, listening.

"Don't come any closer!" Lawrence yelled from behind a closed door upstairs. "The police are on their way!"

Fuck!

He didn't have long. Beachfront addresses got top priority. "I just have a few questions, Mr. Kampf."

"Leave now. I don't want any trouble."

"Too late, son. Trouble is coming your way if you don't answer my questions."

He ran up the stairs making as little noise as possible, then arrived at Lawrence's room. If the man was holding a gun, there was an excellent chance he'd shoot through the door if he heard anything.

Jasper stayed quiet, waiting for Lawrence to make the next move, hoping like hell that the sheriff's office wasn't

moving in. In a house like this, they might roll in silent, not wanting to spook the invader — meaning that Jasper would be trapped if he didn't get out in time.

What would Jordyn do if he got arrested and never came back? He didn't want her growing up without a father.

Jasper closed his eyes and touched the door, trying to get a flash of something. He'd never understood his psychic gifts or why they failed to work more often than not. Nor did he understand why Jordyn had been getting more visions than him. Was it that he'd neglected his powers, cursed them for so long after his wife died that they just stopped coming?

Whatever the case, he needed something now.

Come on. Just lemme know how long I have before the deputies are barging in.

Something! Anything!

Jasper didn't get a vision, so much as a flash of something he'd barely noticed while running past the kitchen — a cell phone next to the stove.

And then he sensed Lawrence's panic on the other side of the door. He'd run upstairs before getting the phone. And whatever room he was in now didn't have one.

Jasper closed his eyes, pressing his hand harder against the door.

He got a sense of Lawrence on the other side, pistol shaking in his hand. Heart racing.

Jasper eased into the hallway, ducked, then said, "You ever shoot a man, Mr. Kampf?"

"I will shoot you! I swear to Christ."

"I don't think you will. And by the way, I've got your phone. So unless you have one in there, and we both know you don't, nobody's coming to save you."

"You come in here, and I will shoot your fucking ass!"

"Oh, I believe you will shoot. But here's the thing, Mr. Kampf, I've got a knife. And I know the old saying about bringing a knife to a gunfight, but I guarantee that after you miss your first two or three shots, I will be on you, my blade buried in your stomach in seconds. And you will bleed out, my friend. Or … we could talk."

Silence.

"Talk through the door," he finally said. "What do you want?"

"I want to know where Jessi Price is."

More silence. Then, "I don't know what you're talking about! Get outta here."

"I suppose you don't know about Dodd's escape, either?"

"I don't know what you're talking about. Leave here now, while you still can."

"I've got a better idea. Why don't I call the sheriff's department. I'll tell them all about Cadillac Taylor and the mercenaries you paid off."

A gunshot ripped through the wall, thunder reverberating through the upstairs hall.

Jasper ducked.

The door opened.

Lawrence came out, gun drawn, aiming straight at Jasper.

Jasper leapt up.

The gun fired again. The sound was like someone clapping hard on his eardrums.

Jasper slammed into the man with his full weight, shoving Lawrence backward and falling atop him. The gun slid from his hand. The lawyer's eyes bulged as he desperately reached for it.

Jasper had his blade at the man's flabby neck.

"One move and I slice your throat. You understand

me?"

Lawrence froze, staring up at Jasper. "Y-y-yes."

"Good. Now I want info. Where is Jessi Price?"

"I don't know. Someone paid me to have Cadillac get her."

"I want names." Jasper pressed the blade into his fatty flesh.

"I don't know any names!"

"Where is Paul Dodd?"

"I don't know. Someone called me, said I'd better do it or they'd release some sensitive information they had on me. They wired three hundred grand into an offshore account. I paid Cadillac from that. We've worked together before. The person who hired me was in contact with Cadillac directly. I was out of the picture."

Jasper stared down. "For a lawyer, you're a shitty liar."

"I swear! I don't fucking know!"

"Then you're no good to me." Jasper pressed the knife until blood beaded the blade.

"I'll give you Cadillac's address. Talk to him. I'll give it to you if you let me go. Come on, brother."

Jasper laughed at the obscenely wealthy, absurdly criminal, and extremely white man trying to use the word "brother" with him. He released the pressure but didn't remove the blade from his neck.

"Tell me now."

"It's in my phone, for Christ's sake."

"All right, Mr. Kampf, let's go get your phone," Jasper said, slowly standing. "But you do *anything* I don't like, and I will cut you into bacon. You feel me, *brother?*"

Lawrence nodded.

The lawyer stood and put a hand on his neck. A minor cut, but you'd have thought Jasper flayed him. "You slit my throat!"

"You'll be fine. Don't be such a pussy."

Jasper followed Lawrence downstairs, then told him to pick up his phone, and get the info.

Meanwhile, he stood behind the lawyer, blade to his neck, watching the man's every move.

He entered his code on the phone, 1-1-7-0, pulled up his contacts, then navigated to Keisha Brown, with a St. Augustine address and number.

"That's Cadillac's girlfriend, Keisha. When he goes dark, that's the only way to reach him."

"And he'll know where Jessi and Paul are?"

"Yes, I swear."

"If he doesn't, I'll be back to kill you."

"Okay!"

Jasper slowly withdrew the blade. He stopped before leaving the kitchen and turned around.

"Why the hell would you facilitate the kidnapping of a child?"

Lawrence, putting a wad of paper towels against his neck, looked confused. "I already told you, they had shit on me."

"What?"

"I'm not telling *you*."

"*Tell me*," Jasper said, his voice deep, as he took a step closer.

"It's nothing. Just some hooker I got photographed with."

"And for that, you were willing to kidnap a young girl and free a serial killing child rapist?"

"I'm not the bad guy, here!"

Jasper darted over and plunged his blade into the man's flabby gut. "I think you are."

Lawrence tried to cry out, but Jasper put a gloved hand over his mouth, hard, and kept cutting the bacon.

Chapter 21 - Paul Dodd

PAUL ENTERED JESSI'S ROOM, hardly able to believe she was sharing paradise with him. A part of him was aroused, looking forward to their time together, though he wasn't sure if he was ready for sex just yet. His body was still so battered and bruised.

"If you need anything, call," Daniel said with the cordiality of a man working the Four Seasons rather than someone inviting him to visit a pre-pubescent prisoner.

"Thank you," Paul said.

Daniel closed the door behind them.

Jessi was sitting up in bed, wearing a pretty white dress, a bow in her hair, face painted with garish makeup and bright red lipstick. Like a harlot. Not his style, or Jessi's. The whole thing felt *off*.

She was staring at him, blank-eyed.

He slowly approached, not wanting to frighten her, but mostly not wanting her to scream or come at him. He could defend himself from a child but didn't want to hurt her.

Her pupils were large, her eyes glassy.

What had they given her? Heroin? Rohypnol? Some cocktail he wasn't familiar with?

He inched closer to the edge of her bed, waiting for some response, for her to realize he was there. But she was staring right through him, either without recognition, or no longer able to care. In this state, she was only a shell, and Paul felt a profound sadness to see her like this.

He sat on the bed beside her, reached out and touched her cheek.

She didn't move an inch. But tears still gathered in the corner of her left eye.

"You poor thing. What did they do to you?"

Still nothing. The tear trickled down her cheek.

"I'm sorry, Jessi. I had nothing to do with this. I didn't ask them to take you."

Another tear, now down the other cheek. Her lip trembled.

She was cracking, and Paul could no longer take it. He stood, went to the door, and banged until Daniel finally opened it.

"What the hell did you do to her?"

"Pardon me?" Daniel looked past Paul toward Jessi. "Is she okay?"

"No, she's not *okay*. She's drugged to hell, man. She's practically catatonic."

"Oh," Daniel said, sounding relieved. "She'll be fine. We had to give her something because she was not taking this very well."

"You don't say," Paul said, annoyed. "Stop giving her that shit."

"Well, the other option was to tie and gag her. She was making too much noise. That tends to hamper the enjoyment of our guests."

"I want to talk to Madam."

"One moment." Daniel pulled a phone from his pocket and made a call. "Yes, he'd like to see her again. No, I don't think he's happy with her condition. Too medicated … Yes … Yes. Okay."

He put his phone away. "This way."

He led Paul back to Madam Pandora's room, then left the two of them to talk.

She was sitting at her desk, same as before. Paul wondered if she ran this place or managed it for someone worse.

"I understand you're not pleased with our gift?"

"She's not herself. She's fucked up on whatever you've got her on."

"I apologize. We were merely trying to be merciful. There are two ways to break a girl — violence or drugs. We figured the less bruising option would be best, but we can adjust."

"No," Paul said, disgusted by the woman's nonchalance at torturing a child. "Aren't there any other options?"

"We could lower the dosage, but if she gets out of hand, we'll have to consider the first method."

"Fine," Paul said.

Madam looked at him, her head tilted ever so, a slight smile playing at the corners of her mouth. "Interesting."

"What?"

"May I be frank?"

"Yes," he said, curious.

"Well, according to your dossier, you've raped and murdered girls. And yet you blanch when we threaten violence against this one. Why is that? Is she special to you?"

Paul weighed his answer. If he said Jessi was special, they could use that as leverage against him. And that could be useful, because in the end, she wasn't. While he didn't

want to harm her, nor did he take particular delight in seeing her in pain, he didn't truly care one way or another about her.

If he gave the impression that he did, that might keep them from seeking other forms of leverage that *would* force him to do what they want. If these people thought nothing of hurting an innocent child, surely they'd not think twice about hurting him or going after *his* daughter.

"Yes, she's special. And I don't care to see her in this state, like some common whore."

Madam nodded. "I understand and apologize for your experience. You should find her closer to normal tomorrow. I promise we won't hurt her, but we may need drugs again if she becomes a threat to our peace."

"Understood."

"Good. Now, about that other thing. Have you considered our request?"

"The safe deposit box?"

"Yes."

"I have. And I'm game, under one more condition."

Her gaze narrowed on him, and he was fairly certain she was pissed beneath her calm facade. The smile left for beat before returning. "Yes?"

"I'm not sure how you managed to get Jessi, but I'm guessing this next request will be easier."

"Go on."

"I want Mallory Black."

Chapter 22 - Mallory Black

MAL WOKE up to a ringing doorbell, looked out her bedroom window, and saw the Sheriff's SUV parked outside.

She grabbed her empty bottle of pills off the ground, hid it in her nightstand drawer, tied her hair back in a ponytail, then went downstairs and opened the door.

"Hello, Mal," Gloria said. "May I come in?"

"Sure, but the place is a bit of a mess. Haven't been staying here for months."

She led Gloria to the dining room table and asked her if she wanted a drink. When the offer was declined, Mal grabbed a cold Diet Coke from the fridge and swallowed some, hoping it masked her morning breath a bit as she took a seat across from her boss.

"So, what brings you by?"

"You've been cleared."

"What?"

"We'll be doing a press release at five. You officially start back on Monday."

"Thank you." Mal was relieved but felt like there was something the sheriff still had to say. "But …?"

"But we'll need you to get counseling and submit to routine drug tests for the next year."

"That's bullshit."

"I need something to show that you're under control."

"I haven't done anything like this in nearly a year!"

"What about last night?"

"What about last night?"

"I heard about your run-in with Cameron Ford at Grommet's."

"It was hardly a *run-in*. I saw them and said hi."

Gloria rolled her eyes. "And you threatened them?"

"I did *not* threaten them. And by the way, who the hell told you this?"

"It was in the Gossip Corner on Creek County Confidential."

"That little bitch needs his website DDOSd. Did he happen to mention that he was having dinner with Merle Fucking Truman? I bet he didn't write that in his bitch-ass column."

"Maybe he was doing a story on Truman? Or he's a client that advertises on Cameron's website?"

Mal was a decibel from yelling. "Or maybe they're meeting so Truman can give Cameron his new instructions from Barry!"

"Even so, you can't keep getting into situations like this."

"I said hi. Believe me, if I wanted a situation, Cameron wouldn't be able to type his lies with two broken hands."

"And *that* is what I'm talking about!" Gloria slammed a palm on the table. "You can't say shit like that."

"Oh, come on. Where did your sense of humor go,

Gloria? You used to talk trash with the best of them. You used to *like it* when I said shit about these cocksuckers."

"Yeah, that was before you were on video beating the crap outta guys. Listen, Mal, I don't need to tell you that the easiest thing for me to do would be leave you out in the cold. That would be the *safe* thing for my reelection in November. I'm doing the right thing instead. But I need you to meet me half-way. Can you do that?"

Mal sighed. "Yes, boss. I'll be a good girl."

"I can't tell if you're being a smart ass or serious."

Mal considered joking, but didn't. "I'm serious. I want to come back. I can't do shit from here, and the longer Jessi's gone and Paul is in the wind, the more dangerous this world is."

"Agreed. Give HR a call and they'll tell you where to go for your drug test."

"Okay. Any chance I can go into the office? Get a head start?"

"Wait until Monday. We've got this until then."

Mal fought to keep her disappointment from her expression and voice. "Yes, ma'am."

AFTER GLORIA LEFT, Mal made something to eat. The only thing in the house worth cooking was chicken noodle soup, so she was sitting at the kitchen table and eating the slop while scrolling through her personal messages. She saw old texts from Ray, asking her to call.

It'd been more than a week since the last one. She'd forgotten to call back, as she'd been busy with the Chloe Conlan case and then the recent madness with Jessi.

Mal dialed, readying her apology for taking so long. She barely started before he said, "Let's not do this."

"What?"

"I don't need to hear the apologies and details of whatever case you're working on. It's fine, Mallory."

"Um, okay," she said, confused by his bitterness. "So, you called?"

"Yeah, I just wanted to talk to you before I left."

"Left. Where are you going?"

"Already gone. I went to New York."

"What? New York? Why?"

"Yeah, I needed a reset. Too many reminders back there. And you know what, I'm happy now."

Mal was pissed, though she wasn't entirely sure why. That he'd left without waiting to say goodbye? Or that he felt he could just forget everything they had together, the *daughter* they shared, by packing up and heading north?

She tried to mask her rancor. She wanted Ray to be happy, even if that meant leaving her behind. "Well, congratulations."

"Thank you. It feels good. You should try it."

"Try what?"

"Starting over."

"You know it's not that easy for me."

"I know you're not making it easy. You *choose* to stay there, in that damned house, stuck in the past. You have a choice. You can be happy if you *want* to be."

Mal bit her tongue, trying not to blast back.

Then he sighed, nice and long. "You know what, never mind. I don't feel like fighting. That's another thing I don't miss. Goodbye, Mal."

And just like that he hung up.

She stared at the phone, still feeling the slap.

Chapter 23 - Jasper Parish

AFTER RANSACKING THE PLACE, Jasper took the lawyer's wallet, phone, laptop, two iPads, and a thumb drive, hoping something would help him find Jessi and Dodd.

He thought about handing them over to Mal and letting the Feds' forensics crew have at it, but that would more or less implicate him in Kampf's death. Besides, he had someone who could do the job quicker.

He pulled up to the rundown two-story tenement in the middle of the Butler projects.

Jordyn looked at Jasper, her eyes big as she surveyed the parking lot filled with young men eying their car with hardening stares. "Um, Dad, why are we here?"

"Seeing Spider."

"Spider? Who the hell is Spider?"

"You'll see."

Jasper opened the trunk and grabbed the duffel filled with the lawyer's electronics. There were too many eyes, assessing him as a threat. He'd never been to Spider's. Their prior meetings had all been on the phone or at other locations.

Jordyn whispered, "Are we safe?"

"Relax, we're fine."

Jasper closed the trunk and approached the entrance. He was stopped by a young, muscular teen in a skull cap and a tee shirt two sizes too small.

"Who you here to see, Pops?" His cold, dark eyes narrowed on Jasper. No doubt he was packing and would think nothing of shooting him on the spot if he deemed this visitor a threat.

"I'm here to see Spider."

"Whatchya got in the bag?"

"That's between me and Spider."

He eyed Jasper up and down again. Then he grabbed his phone and dialed. "Yo, Spider, some old fool is here to see you … What's your name, Pops?"

"Professor Xavier," Jasper said.

"He says he's some professor, Xavier or some shit. You know this clown?"

The man looked disappointed in the answer, said "Okay," then led them inside and up the stairs to the last apartment on the left.

The man knocked twice, waited, then beat the wood another three times. Jasper could hear EDM thumping on the other side. The door buzzed open.

"This way, professor," the man said, eyeballing Jasper the whole way.

As run-down and dirty as the building's exterior was, the inside of Spider's unit was its opposite, a tech junkie's version of a minimalist.

"Hold up a minute," Spider shouted from the back, though she was hard to hear over the music.

The volume fell, and Jasper turned his attention to the back room.

The door opened. Behind Spider, he spied shelves full

of boxes and parts. She was carrying an ancient looking computer, rolling her wheelchair into the living room.

She looked up at Jasper with a giant smile and bright green eyes. "Finally came by to see the place?"

Spider set her computer on the ground, then opened her arms for a hug.

Jasper embraced her, awkwardly enough to make her laugh.

"So damned stiff, man. You need to lighten the eff up."

Spider, real name Felicia Borrego, was a half-Cuban half-Jamaican, eighteen-year-old girl, and the sole survivor of a car crash that killed both her parents five years ago. In addition to losing the use of her legs, she had a vicious scar on her forehead that she did nothing to hide. Whether using colored extensions, or putting her hair in neat pigtails like today, Spider never hid her face. Jasper had rescued her from some trouble in a foster home and recognized that her talents would be put to better use working for him.

"Yeah, well I'm old and set in my ways. And yes, nice place, though I still don't know why you want to live here. I offered you a dozen better options in much better — *safer* — neighborhoods."

"I fit in here. People always lookin' at me weird in those other places. Here I'm one of them."

"Maybe they don't identify with you so much as need you, thanks to the odd job for dealers or gangsters? How long before that blows up?"

"You come to lecture me, Professor, or you need some help?"

Jordyn smiled. "She told you, Dad."

Jasper shot his daughter a look and was about to introduce her to Spider, but then he remembered.

"So, whachya' got?"

Jasper explained the situation. Discretion was a given, or else he wouldn't be here.

"Let's see what we're working with." Spider took the duffel from Jasper and set it on her L-shaped desk, long enough to occupy the entire right and back walls of the living room, where most people might put a sectional couch.

Instead she had tables lined with monitors and various shelves and drawers loaded with the tools of her trade.

She opened the laptop, put blue tape over the camera, and turned it on.

"Password protected, but I'll get around it," she said before diving deeper into the bag and removing the phone and thumb drive.

"Code is 1-1-7-0 on the phone," Jasper said. "See what you can get from it, any associated accounts, websites, everything."

"Gotcha." She punched in the same password on the tablets, but it didn't work. "The iPads might take a little longer, but I don't anticipate any problems with the other stuff. Most folks around here aren't so savvy with the encryption."

"Whatever you can get, fast as you can get it. Jessi Price is counting on us."

"Gotcha, Professor, I won't rest until I'm done."

"Thank you. And Spider?"

"Yeah?"

"I need one more thing before I go."

Chapter 24 - Jasper Parish

As JASPER DROVE to Cadillac's St. Augustine address, Jordyn stared out the window, deep in thought.

"Whatcha thinkin' about?"

"About Ophelia and Alicia," Jordyn said. "And how much of a shame it is that things didn't work out. Do you think you'll ever see her again?"

"I carry a shit storm wherever I go. It's probably best to steer clear of everyone."

"That wasn't your fault. Her sister was with those meth dealers. They would've come around whether you were there or not. Hell, maybe they would've killed them all if you hadn't been."

"Maybe, maybe not."

"No maybes about it. You can't blame yourself for that, Dad. It's not on you."

"Well, either way, now they see what I really am. Ain't nobody wanna be with someone like this."

"You're not a *bad* guy."

"I think some people would argue."

"Well, *I* don't think you're bad."

"Either way, as long as I do stuff like this, I can't have a normal life. It isn't fair to the people around me."

"Then maybe it's time to give up on this life. Let the cops do their job."

"No. Even if they managed to bring in the lawyer, he wouldn't have said a word. I got info they couldn't, or wouldn't, be able to get. So, yeah, I think they need my help. Same for Jessi and Mallory."

"Okay, but what about after this is all over? What do you think will happen then? That Detective Black will be your buddy, you two driving around solving cases together? Do you think this is a TV show? The minute this is over, assuming either she or Jessi make it out alive, she *will* arrest you."

"What is it with you and her? You never did like her, did you?"

"I like her fine. But she's a cop, Dad. And it's her job to stop people like you, even if you're right."

"So, what, now you don't believe in my mission?"

"I didn't say that. I just think it's time to stop and do something else with your life. You can't keep on like this forever." Jordyn laughed. "You sure as hell ain't getting any younger."

"What am I supposed to do, huh?"

"I don't know, maybe try and be happy? You deserve it after what happened to Mom, and …"

"What?"

"Nothing."

"No, I want to know what."

"Well, what happened to me."

"What are you talking about?" She was looking away like it was something he ought to know. Something she'd told him before. Now her feelings would be hurt that he didn't remember.

"Come on, Dad. You know what I'm talking about."

"No, I don't." He pulled over then into a Publix parking lot. "What are you talking about?"

"Never mind," she said, crossing her arms, reminding him again of Mallory.

"I'm dead, Dad. You do remember, don't you?"

And then, just like that, he did.

Yet, she was still next to him in the car. Still looking at him.

Somehow.

"I … I know you're dead. Sometimes, I just … I forget is all."

"And Mom is dead, too."

"I know, Jordyn. I remember."

"Are you taking your meds?"

"You know the answer to that. You're here, aren't you?"

"Listen, Dad. I love that we're still talking. And that I'm still so much in your heart. But maybe I'm holding you back from being happy or having a normal life."

"Don't say that."

"Maybe that's why Mom doesn't come around. Maybe she knows it was hurting you."

"I can't have a normal life. I can't just sit by and know the things I know without doing anything. The meds dull my gift, and they keep you away. Why would I ever give up on that?"

"Because this won't end well for you."

"What do you mean?"

"Come on, Dad. I know the dreams you've been having. The man with the machete. I've been having them, too. Please stop, before it's too late."

He stared out the window, watching a young mother

wrangle two toddlers into a car-shaped shopping cart, wondering if Jordyn had a point.

"So, what do I do? Just take my meds and live a normal life? Never see you or Mom again?"

"We'll see each other, either here or in Heaven."

"Heaven?" he laughed. "You think I'm going to Heaven after all I've done?"

"There's still time to make everything right."

He wanted to ask Jordyn if she made it to Heaven. He knew what the Bible said about suicides going to Hell and hated the thought of his sweet little girl being tortured for an eternity. If there was a God, Jasper hoped He would take mercy on those who killed themselves. For hadn't they already suffered in life?

But he didn't want to upset Jordyn. Besides, if she were a figment of his imagination, a split personality, or some other personification of him, then she wouldn't know Jordyn's fate.

But if she were really here, a ghost, as he preferred to believe, then perhaps she wasn't anywhere yet. Neither Heaven nor Hell. Maybe there was nowhere to go, except for here.

"Maybe. After this case is over. But for now, Jessi and Mallory need me. They need *us*. Okay?"

Jordyn nodded, and Jasper put the car back into motion.

Chapter 25 - Jasper Parish

JASPER ARRIVED at the address for Keisha Brown, a small ranch-style house in a rundown area just outside the historic district.

"How do I look?" he asked Jordyn, smoothing out his suit jacket and donning a charcoal fedora.

"Like you're selling God."

"Good." He got out of the car, patted the holster under his jacket, then headed toward the front door. The patchy yard was filled with weeds, a couple of small, slightly rusted bikes, a faded basketball, and other detritus of childhood and neglect.

He retrieved an envelope from his pocket and knocked.

A young woman answered the door wearing a half-shirt, tight yoga pants, curlers in her hair, and a scowl. Behind her stood two little kids — a boy around three and a girl maybe a year older. "Yeah?"

"Got a job for Cadillac."

She looked Jasper up and down. "I don't know you. Why you comin' 'round here?"

He opened his envelope and showed her the bills. "There's five grand here. Another ten on completion."

"Who the hell are you?" Her nose twitched, involuntary, like it was grabbing a scent.

"Name's John Dennings. A mutual friend gave me Cadillac's info, said he was a man who could get stuff done. Tell me I'm wrong, and I'll find someone else."

Jasper turned and took two steps toward his car.

"Hold up," she said. "What's the job?"

Jasper stifled a smile and turned back around.

Chapter 26 - Jasper Parish

Jasper got back in the car, drove to a nearby shopping center, stopped the vehicle, pulled out the cell phone that Spider had cloned Keisha's number to, and waited.

"So, let me get this straight," Jordyn said. "Spider can clone anyone's number?"

"Pretty much," Jasper said. "She explained it to me once. Something about a known vulnerability in most phones, but it's not fixed because it's a backdoor that the government uses to spy on people. Once we have his number, we can track him and maybe clone his phone."

"You believe her?"

"I don't know. She subscribes to a lot of crazy shit. I know when I was working on the force we didn't have tools like this, but who knows what the NSA, CIA, and other agencies can do these days."

It didn't take long for Keisha to call Cadillac and tell him of the curious job offer from "the cat in the wool hat."

Cadillac said, "I don't know this dude. What's the job?"

"A simple heist. Said some rich dude is staying at a

nearby hotel. Said he's got no security and is an easy mark. Dude can't do it himself because it's his business partner."

"Hmm, I dunno. You get his number?"

"Yeah."

"'K, we can talk about this later. Right now, I've gotta deliver the package."

"All right, honey. When you coming home?"

"Should be tonight. Miss you."

"Miss you, too. Love you."

They hung up.

"Delivering a package?" Jasper wondered aloud.

He set down the cloned phone, then called Spider and gave her Cadillac's number.

"I'll hit you in a few with his location history," she promised.

Jasper felt something gnawing at his gut, like something awful was about to happen. The same feeling he got in the haze of an unclear vision, a vague threat he couldn't nail down. That feeling of waiting, but not knowing where or when the evil might strike.

He looked at Jordyn. "You getting any visions?"

She shook her head. But he could tell from her pained expression that she shared his unease.

A text came through on Jasper's phone — a list of locations stretching back to this morning.

And as he went through it, his blood ran cold.

"Oh, no."

Chapter 27 - Mallory Black

MAL STARED AT THE TV, watching Ashley at age three, giggling a raspy laugh as her mother tickled her.

"Stop it, Mommy!"

Mal would stop, then Ashley would say, "Again!"

Mal tickled her, and so it went for several minutes until the video cut to Ashley pointing to her picture book. "He still doesn't see the birdie on his head!"

Mal wiped tears from her eyes as she finished her wine, then stopped the video and stood. She grabbed her gun from beside her on the couch, carried it with her to the bathroom, and set it on the sink counter. She looked at herself in the mirror and laughed. "Getting drunk in the middle of the day watching videos of Ashley is *not* helping you find Jessi."

But what else could she do?

She thought about calling Colleen but couldn't deal with her in such a hopeless mood. Besides, she was sure that Mike, and likely an FBI agent or two, were giving Colleen the necessary attention, lying to buoy her spirits. And Mal definitely wasn't in the mood to lie.

All she could think about was the cold hard truth — the longer Jessi was missing, the less likely they were to find her alive. And that didn't even take into account the odds when a super predator like Paul Dodd pursued a girl he had already victimized.

She stared in the mirror, wishing it were a magical portal to look in on Dodd. "What are you doing to her, you sick bastard?"

Breaking glass downstairs snapped Mal to attention. She grabbed her gun and went to the stairs, listening as she slowly descended.

Did a glass fall? Or was Dodd coming to get her?

Let him fucking come!

I've got something for you!

Mal aimed her gun as she reached the bottom floor, searching for the noise, scanning every corner, checking the doors.

The front door was open.

Fuck!

Her shoulders tightened. So did her grip as she strained to hear movement.

Something hit the ground in front of her with a hard thud, then rolled.

She looked down to see a grenade, then bolted toward the door, to put as much distance between herself and the explosion. But the detonation never came.

Instead, another grenade landed at her feet, and gas spilled out, filling her field of vision.

No!

She choked on the smoke, her eyes stinging. Then she covered her mouth and crawled toward the door.

But Mal was disoriented and had lost the exit behind a wall of smoke.

She couldn't move at all.
And then she fell.

Chapter 28 - Jasper Parish

JASPER PULLED up behind Mal's car in the driveway, walked past it, then knocked on her front door.

No response.

He stared at the broken window leading to her living room, wondering if someone had thrown a rock through, or maybe taken a shot.

He'd called her twice on the drive over, even left a warning, but got only silence in return.

His every nerve was on edge 'as he listened for any sound coming from inside the house. If they'd come and taken her, they were probably long gone, but you never knew for sure.

He tried the doorknob. Unlocked.

Jasper didn't bother turning around to make sure no neighbors were walking by or watching. Best to act like he belonged.

He went inside, saying, "Hello, Mallory" as he went, acting as if she'd let him in.

He closed the door and drew his gun. "Mallory?"

Jordyn was behind him, her eyes wide, listening intently.

"You feel anything?"

She walked toward the center of the room then knelt down, closed her eyes, and touched the floor. A moment later, she looked up at him. "There were three men here. They took her."

"Do you know where?"

She squeezed her eyes tighter, then stood, walking around the living room with her eyes closed, waiting for something to come.

He watched, helplessly, hoping she'd picked up on something useful.

After a long moment, she opened her eyes and shook her head.

"Shit."

Jasper was about to head upstairs, but his phone rang first. The burner whose number he'd given to Cadillac's girlfriend. He disguised his voice and answered.

"Cadillac?"

"Yeah, who is this?"

"John Dennings. A friend gave me your info. Said you could help me."

"Yeah? What friend?"

Jasper looked at Jordyn. She whispered, "Percy."

"Percy," Jasper repeated, taking a deep breath as he waited to hear if the name checked out. Cadillac would either continue the conversation or hang up and go into hiding.

"What's the job?"

Jasper smiled as they made plans to meet tonight.

Chapter 29 - Jasper Parish

JORDYN COULDN'T STOP LAUGHING in the passenger seat, staring at her father's disguise. "You look ridiculous!"

Jasper was wearing an oversized brown suit from the 70s, an equally out-of-style fedora, a gray afro wig, and wire-rimmed glasses.

"Oh, you're just mad I didn't take your advice and dress in a fat suit and a dress."

"Hey, it works for Tyler Perry."

"This will work fine," he said, driving.

Jasper had arranged to meet Cadillac at a bar near his place, on his turf, to put him at ease. But Jasper had no intention of meeting him there.

Instead, he called Spider and had her track Cadillac's location, figuring he wasn't about to head back to his girlfriend's house until he knew more about the stranger wanting to hire him. For all he knew, the cops were onto him, so Cadillac would find someplace to lay low until after the meet.

Fortunately, that meant a squat one-story fleabag motel not too far from his girlfriend's place, just off the highway.

The Breezy Motor Lodge wasn't yet exclusively a den of drugs and prostitution, but it was barely hanging on in the battle against time and decay. Chipped paint, a crumbling parking lot, and lights in its sign that would never be fixed all signaled the end as nigh.

A sign on a fence announced the pool was closed and management was "sorry for the inconvenience." But if Jasper was a betting man, he'd wager his house or more that the pool hadn't seen service in a year or longer.

He drove through the parking lot, looking for Cadillac's car. Spider had given him the make and model, a brand new black Mercedes-Benz CLS, easily the nicest car that would be in this place. He passed a big rig and its trailer, then a few campers as he made his way through the lot. Finally found Cadillac's Mercedes parked at the far end, in front of the farthest block of rooms in the corner of the L-shaped motel.

He wondered if Cadillac would park in front of or away from his room. Likely the latter as a matter of precaution, so he could be in any of the L's corner quarters.

Jasper parked to the left of Cadillac's car, so close that he hit the Mercedes hard enough to trigger the alarm. He hunched over, making himself appear as old as possible, squinting at Cadillac's car, then around at the rooms, looking lost.

One of the doors burst open, and Cadillac came running out in sweat pants and a tee shirt, his face twisted in anger. "What the fuck?"

The man was a house. Jasper hoped he'd never have to fight him. Cadillac pressed his key fob to silence the alarm.

"Sorry," Jasper said in his best frail, old man's voice as Cadillac drew closer, focused on the damage to his car.

Cadillac glared at him, then bent to inspect the dent in his door. "You know how much this shit is gonna c—"

Jasper pressed the pistol into Cadillac's back. "Walk slowly back to your room. We need to talk. Do anything stupid, and I put you down right here. You understand?"

Cadillac swallowed, nodded, not turning back to see the old man with the suddenly young voice who had clearly outsmarted him.

They walked to his room, Jasper keeping the gun just out of sight.

He ordered Cadillac to sit on the bed. Jordyn entered the room behind him, wearing a pink and purple ski mask pulled low over her face. Jasper closed the door.

Cadillac was staring right at him. "You John Dennings?"

"I'm the one asking questions. You're the one answering. Understand?"

Cadillac said nothing, glaring at Jasper.

He aimed his pistol so that Cadillac could appreciate the suppressor. "I need to repeat myself?"

Cadillac nodded his head.

"Good. Where did you take Jessi Price?"

Cadillac's eyes widened. He started to stand.

Jasper fired into his left foot.

Cadillac fell back to the bed, crying out as he looked down to survey the damage.

"Quiet! I didn't hit anything critical. But the next one goes into your gut, heart, or head."

Cadillac clenched his fists, gritting his teeth through the pain.

"Where did you take Jessi Price?"

"You a cop?"

Jasper laughed. "What do you think?"

"Why you looking for her?"

"I might ask why the hell you're kidnapping kids. Seems a bit of a reach, even for a low-level enforcer such as yourself."

Calling him by his real name had almost the same effect as mentioning Jessi. His eyes narrowed in on Jasper, realizing that he was well and truly fucked. "What the hell you know about me?"

"I know you're not a kidnapper. You used to be a good guy, despite working for Lil' Tony. And you'd hate for Curtis Johnson to find out where you've run off to."

"What do you want?"

"I want to know where you took Jessi."

"You ain't gonna get her back."

"Why not?" Jasper asked, fearing that she was already dead.

"She's not here."

"Where is she?"

"Mexico."

"What?"

"Listen, man, I don't know all the details. I got hired to get and deliver her. That's all I'm saying."

"I don't think you understand how this works. I ask questions, you give me *all* the answers."

"I tell you everything, and I'm good as dead."

"You think you're walking out of here if you don't?"

Cadillac squeezed his eyes tight. Jasper wasn't sure if he was going to break down and cry, or if he was trying to get through the pain. "I didn't want to take that girl. I didn't have no choice."

"Why?"

"You don't know these people. They're powerful. They threatened to reach out to Curtis if I didn't do the job. They threatened Keisha and the kids."

"Who are *they?*"

Cadillac shook his head. "Nope. You may as well just shoot me."

"What if I could help you?"

Cadillac laughed. "Help me what?"

"Get out from under them?"

"How you gonna do that? You got an army?"

Jasper reached into his coat, peeled off one of the plastic-wrapped sheets of money he'd buried in a large hidden pocket, and threw it at Cadillac.

"There's a hundred grand there. All legit. And another hundred-fifty waiting for you after I get the girl back. I'll get new IDs for you, your girl, and the kids. You can go away and start over. Again."

Cadillac stared at the money, then at Jasper. "Who the hell are you?"

"A friend of Lenny Barnes. He vouches for you doing the right thing."

"Lenny? Man, I ain't seen that cat in forever. Thought he died. Did he send you?"

Jasper nodded. "Some people thought you were dead, too. Now tell me who hired you."

"For real? You a friend of Lenny's?"

Jasper nodded. "He says you could've been the next Alonzo Mourning or Shaq."

Cadillac laughed, wiping tears from his eyes. "Man, he always saw more in me than I did."

"Me, too," Jasper confessed.

Cadillac stared at him for a long moment, then said, "BlackBriar hired me."

"BlackBriar? I thought they fired you."

"Yeah, they did. *Officially*, anyway. But that's just part of the recruitment process for their shady side deals, or what I call their *real* business."

"What's their *real* business?"

Cadillac laughed. "Drugs, sex slavery, extortion, and that's just for starters. Funny. I thought I finally got a legit job, was turning my life around. But it turns out the new boss is same as the old one."

"And why did they want Jessi?"

"I dunno, man."

Jasper watched Cadillac through his silence, waiting to see if he'd volunteer details about Mallory. He wasn't sure that he'd let the man live if he didn't.

"Don't know why we took the cop either," he finally said.

"What cop?" Jasper asked, playing dumb.

"Mallory Black. I dunno. Seemed almost personal."

"And where is she going?"

"Mexico, too, I think."

"And you don't know why?"

"Fuck." Cadillac shook his head. "In for a penny, may as well tell you all of it."

"Good idea."

"I wasn't on this particular gig, but one of my buddies said he was on that job to break that pedophile Paul Dodd out of custody."

"And is he also in Mexico?"

"I don't know, but if I had to guess, then yeah. And I didn't connect the dots at the time, Price and Dodd, and their ... history."

"Why did you think you were taking her? You kidnap kids so often that you didn't think to ask?"

"No, man. This was the first. I swear. I was only there as backup. I didn't even know the whole job until right before we left. And I didn't know the girl's name at all until I saw it on the news. I figured it was some custody thing. BlackBriar works for rich folks who buy whatever the law can't or won't give them."

Jasper sighed, long and deep. "Where is Black now?"

"Probably already on a truck to Mexico."

"Thank you for your help, Cadillac." Jasper turned to Jordyn. "You trust him?"

She stared at her father, thinking. "I dunno."

"Who are you talking to?" Cadillac asked.

Jasper held up a finger. *Wait.*

"He did kidnap Jessi. But, at the same time, I believe he didn't know the details. They coerced him into doing the job." Jordyn nodded. "I think he's telling the truth."

Jasper showed Cadillac his phone. "This is my insurance policy against you getting stupid. This has all been recorded. You do anything to stop me, warn your boss, or anything that I or my partners don't like, we'll destroy everything and everyone you've ever known. You understand me?"

Cadillac nodded.

"Good. Now tell me who I should talk to at BlackBriar so I can find out where exactly Jessi and Mallory are."

"Talk to? Like they're just gonna *talk*?"

"I'll find a way. Just give me a name."

"There's two guys who would likely know what you need. Obviously, there's Victor Forbes, and then the second in command, a guy named Anders Martin. He might be your safest bet — he gets drunk at Spanky's every Friday."

"Spanky's?"

"A strip club. The dude has enough to spend every night in the penthouse, but still likes to get his girls from the trailer."

"And he'll know?"

"He runs the day-to-day. Hell, Forbes is hardly ever around. Martin's your best bet, anyway."

Chapter 30 - Jasper Parish

"I DON'T KNOW ABOUT THIS," Jordyn said as Jasper pulled up to the strip club.

He ignored her as his phone rang — Spider.

"It's done," she said.

"And everything went without a hitch?"

"No hitches."

No one was hurt. Jasper exhaled. He hadn't wanted to outsource such a delicate operation, but was pressed for time and lives hung in the balance. "Thanks. I'll be in touch."

He hung up. Jordyn was giving him The Stare.

"What?"

"So, that's how far we've sunk now? To do *that?* I thought we were better than them."

"I don't need guilt trips. I did what I had to."

"Does that make it right?"

"I don't know about right, nor do I care. Not when there's a job to do."

"No matter the cost?"

"Nobody was hurt."

"Yet."

"Do you want to save Jessi and Mallory?"

"Of course I do."

"Well, we're going up against people who don't play fair. People who don't give a damn about the rules. People who will board a school bus and shoot a bus driver and a kid, then kidnap another. So forgive me if I don't feel too bad for bending the rules."

"We don't target innocents. They aren't part of this."

"Sometimes the only way to win a war against bad people is to go further than they will."

Jordyn's eyes widened. "What does that even mean? That now you're willing to kill innocents?"

Jasper didn't answer. She wouldn't like what he had to say. He got out of the car instead. "Wait here."

She didn't argue.

Jasper lowered his Yankees cap and went into Spanky's, an average strip club on a typical Friday night. Filled with a mix of young, drunk college kids; sad old men frittering cash in the vain hopes of impressing young women, or at the very least, getting a happy ending in the back room; the occasional couple out for a night of fun; and the creepy dudes in booths, sitting alone and making deposits into their spank banks for later.

Jasper sat at the bar. A blonde with a fake tan and faker tits said, "Whatcha having, Sweetie?"

He ordered a beer, tipped her well, then turned around, pretending to watch the dancer taking center stage, a short black girl that looked barely older than Jordyn, dressed in a tiny neon pink skirt that matched her lipstick as some idiot rapper throbbed from the speakers.

Jasper scanned the club, searching for his target. After a few minutes, he found Anders sitting by himself at a table near the stage, drinking and chatting with a redheaded

dancer. She was laughing at everything he said, touching his arm, and flirting hard.

"How are you doing, baby?" A young blonde had approached him and spoke in a throaty voice with a thick, Russian accent. She took a seat next to him at the bar. She was in her early twenties, if that, and gorgeous — far too pretty for a dive like this.

What things had gone wrong in her life to have led her here? Had she been tricked into coming, forced to work for the sex industry as so many women in the former Soviet Union and other countries had been?

Or perhaps he had her all wrong. Maybe she was one of the few who liked the job, one of the rare exotic dancers who *was* saving to become a lawyer.

But Jasper had been a cop long enough to know most girls had tragic backgrounds that broke your heart and made you want to punch things.

"Good. And you?"

"Better, now that you're here." She eyed him up and down. "What's your name?"

"Dennis."

She offered him her hand. "I'm Nastya."

He shook it, feeling awkward.

Small talk was high on the list of things Jasper hated. Even higher was the awkward exchanges that could only happen in a place like this, where every word was working to worm its way into his wallet.

The whole thing was sad for everyone involved, and Jasper wished the blonde would just go away.

But as he watched his mark, a second dancer — a tanned Japanese woman in a white bikini — joined Anders at his table. The man looked up, directly toward Jasper.

He didn't turn, as that would give him away. Instead Jasper pretended to be staring center stage. Then he

turned to Nastya and flirted back. She laughed at his dumb joke, so he was blending in.

Nothing to see here, Anders. Just another dude in a seedy club.

Nastya asked Jasper if he'd like a private dance. No, but he wasn't ready for her to leave.

"You want a drink?"

Of course she did. He told her to order whatever she wanted.

The song changed, and the girl on stage was now nude.

Jasper pretended to watch her, though he found her much more attractive in clothes.

He kept an eye on Anders and his pair of strippers. They all stood, then started toward the back room. Jasper turned to Nastya.

"You know what, I think I *will* take that private dance."

She smiled, taking a sip of her drink. It was probably non-alcoholic. Dudes would spend a fortune trying to get a girl drunk, thinking they might be that rare guy who got to take a stripper home — or at least get a blow job in the parking lot.

Nastya led Jasper past a mean-looking bouncer and into a long hall of curtained booths. The empties had their curtains pulled back to red leather love seats and tables big enough for exactly two drinks.

Nine of the booths were occupied. He wondered which one Anders was in.

One of the curtains pushed back as the Japanese girl brushed against it, removing her top. Four booths down and across from Jasper.

Nastya stepped inside, pulled the curtain closed, and sat beside Jasper. "I'll wait for the next song to start." Then she ran her fingers over his chest. "So, what do you do, Dennis?"

Ugh, more small talk.

"Funny you should ask. I help people in bad spots. I'm here to catch a bad man before he hurts someone I love."

She looked confused. He reached into his pants pocket, pulled out a wad of hundreds, and started counting. Fourteen hundred dollars. More in his other pocket.

"I need you to do me a favor. Bring me over to this booth."

"Um, I—"

"Do this, and you can keep the money." Jasper handed her the cash.

Nastya was confused, her hands on the money, not sure what she was agreeing to.

"The man I'm after kidnapped a little girl. I'm trying to get her home. Can you help me? Can you help her mother?"

She nodded, taking the money and stuffing it into her garter belt.

"Let's go." Jasper stood and nodded toward the booth where the dancers were grinding on Anders.

The bouncer glanced at her. She nodded — *everything's cool* — then dipped behind the curtain and pulled Jasper in behind her.

Anders, who had the Japanese dancer on his lap, looked up shocked. "What's going on?"

The dancers looked at Nastya. Jasper handed them both wads of hundreds. "Get lost. Nastya stays."

The women left in a hurry.

"What the hell is this about?" Anders said, starting to stand.

"Sit down, Anders. We need to talk. It's about your family."

"What?" His eyes dilated. Maybe he thought Jasper was a cop, Jasper had that look even in jeans.

He fished the phone from his jacket, pulled up the

video feed, and showed Anders the room with the two people tied to chairs. "My associates have your wife and daughter. If you fail to comply, or they don't hear from me in a timely manner, they'll kill them both."

Anders's eyes went so wide, Jasper thought they might pop right out of his reddening face. "Who the fuck are you?"

"I've come to save the girl you kidnapped. Jessi Price, name ring a bell?"

"I have no idea what you're talking about."

Jasper shook his head. "Wrong answer. Should I text my friends and tell them not to wait? To just go ahead and cut your wife and little girl to pieces now?"

The man obviously wanted to tear Jasper to shreds, or at the very least curse him out, maybe tell him he was a dead motherfucker.

But Jasper tapped the phone's screen, threatening to make good on his promise, and the man could only say, "No!"

"You're going to help me find three people — Jessi Price, Mallory Black, and Paul Dodd. Do you understand?"

Anders nodded.

"Good. Then let's get out of here." Jasper handed Nastya's another wad of cash. "Thank you."

Saturday

Chapter 31 - Jessi Price

JESSI THOUGHT IT WAS MORNING.

The clock read 7:00 a.m., but there were no windows, and she hadn't been allowed outside her room since she got here. She felt closer to normal, at least not as groggy or sleepy as yesterday.

Jessi had a nightmare, but could only remember that it was terrifying and she woke up crying.

She still had no idea who had taken her. Didn't remember much after the bus. They'd given her pills and made her swallow them. Next thing she knew, she was opening her eyes in this room.

The only person she'd seen was a young dark-haired Spanish girl named Lucia. She looked to be in her late teens, maybe early twenties. She told Jessi everything would be okay.

When Jessi asked where her mother was, Lucia said for now, she had to stay here, but she'd return home in time, after they got what they wanted from someone.

She didn't clarify beyond that, other than to remind her, "Everything will be okay."

Jessi's door opened.

Lucia came in holding a tray. "I hope you're hungry today." She smiled and set it on the bed in front of Jessi. There was a bowl of oatmeal, toast, sausage, a cup of milk, and a container of sugar.

"Do you like oatmeal?" Lucia sat at the other end of the bed, like she usually did.

Jessi was confused by her kindness. The others were gruff, from the men who snatched her off the bus to the guy who came in on her first day when she cried out for help. He hit her across the face and said something in a language she didn't understand. But Jessi got the message: *Shut up.*

"Yes, thank you, Miss Lucia." Jessi dipped her spoon into the oatmeal and tasted it. Warm and creamy. Sweet, with a hint of cinnamon. She was either starving, or it was genuinely delicious. Either way, it hit the spot and she scarfed it.

"How are you feeling?" Lucia asked.

"Better. I think the medicine you gave me last night was better."

"You slept through the night?"

"Yes, and I don't feel nearly as groggy today. I can actually think in complete sentences."

"Good."

"I don't want to take any more medicine."

"I'm sorry. You have to … until you go home."

"Why?"

"They want to make sure you don't try to escape. The medicine calms you down."

"When am I going home?"

"I'm not sure. Not too much longer. A few days, I think. But I can't promise. I don't make the decisions. I only work here."

"Why do you work here with these bad people?"

Lucia smiled sadly. "I was born here."

"What?"

"Yes. My mother works here. And I was born here. I grew up here and help out when I can. Especially when we have younger guests."

"What is this place?"

"The less you know the better. Otherwise they might not let you go home."

"Oh." While Jessi wanted to know what and *where* this place was, she didn't want to stay. If she had to choose between getting answers and going home, she'd pick going home twelve times out of ten.

"So, what's it like living here?"

"I don't know what it's like to live anywhere else. I get to spend evenings and weekends with my mom."

"What does she do?"

"She … um, she is like a hostess, I guess."

"Do you have friends? Did you get to play with other kids growing up?"

"Not really. I have some friends, mostly the women who work with Mom. But nobody my age. Every now and then someone like you comes to stay here. So what's it like … back home?"

"I lived in Florida. It's hot. It rains every afternoon in the summer. But it's near the ocean, and sometimes we go to the beach."

"What's the beach like?"

Jessi described the beach, her school, and a dozen other things Lucia had no experience with, including a slew of movies and shows.

"Do you have a lot of friends?"

"A few, though not as many as I had before—" Jessie didn't want to talk about that man or what he'd done to

her. She didn't want Lucia looking at her like the kids at school — with either pity or judgment.

"Before what?" Lucia asked.

Jessi wasn't going to say, but there was a look in Lucia's big brown eyes that promised understanding. That she wouldn't judge. So Jessi told her everything, from how she'd been taken, what Paul had done to her, then how she was saved by a detective and a man in a mask.

Lucia's lips pursed, her eyes wet with tears. "Wow. They didn't tell me."

"Who didn't tell you?"

"Don't worry. Like I said, the less you know, the better."

Lucia looked down at the quilt, her fingers tracing the patterns as if she'd said too much already.

Jessi regretted telling her. Lucia was no longer smiling.

"I'm sorry. I didn't mean to make you sad."

"You sweet thing." Lucia picked up the tray, put it on the dresser, then came over and hugged her tight. Maybe she was a prisoner, too.

"I'm so sorry," she whispered. "You're too young for this."

"Too young for what?" Jessi whispered back.

Lucia pulled away from the embrace and met her eyes. "Listen. Just do whatever they tell you to do. No matter what happens, know that you *will be okay*. That when this is all over, I will help you get better. I promise."

"When *what's* all over?" Jessi asked, fear tightening like a band around her chest.

She looked at the door. She had a flash of *him* walking through it. Looking at her, reaching out and touching her face. "He's here, isn't he? Paul Dodd is here!"

Lucia blinked back tears. "It'll be okay."

Jessi couldn't breathe. Her heart jackhammered. She felt dizzy.

How did he get out of jail? Why was he here? Was he the reason she was here?

Oh, God, what is he going to do to me?

She tried to ask her questions, but Jessi couldn't catch her breath long enough to form words. Her heart galloped so fast. Surely she'd pass out or drop dead.

"You need to calm down. Everything will be okay."

And then Jessi found her voice in a scream.

The door burst open.

Two men in white outfits stormed inside, pushing right past Lucia.

Who are they?

She panicked, crawling backward in her bed, trying to flee, but Jessi was cornered.

They were on her, holding her down.

She couldn't breathe. Or move. She struggled, but they were too strong.

"Be gentle, she's not a threat!" Lucia shouted.

What was she talking about, *not a threat?*

One of the men was holding a needle like they had at the doctor's office. And he was about to inject it into Jessi's arm. She cried out but couldn't stop him.

And then it was in her.

Chapter 32 - Mallory Black

MAL WOKE WITH A SPLITTING HEADACHE, dizzy and cuffed to a bedpost in a dark room.

And she wasn't alone.

She could hear breathing. Mal thought about pretending she was still gassed, but she'd moved enough to surrender that ruse. "Hello?"

No answer.

She strained to see through the darkness, but the room was pitch black. And incredibly cold.

"Hello?"

She wondered if she'd imagined the breathing. But the movement came from up ahead and to the right. Mal braced at the sound of someone approaching.

"Ah, you're up," said a man with a Mexican accent. Based on the sound, he was just inches away.

She flinched, expecting him to touch or hurt her.

A sudden light blinded her, the man shining a flashlight right into her eyes.

It raked her body, up and down, revealing the fancy blue dress that did not belong to her.

"What the hell is going on?" she yelled, not caring if anyone heard her or got pissed off by her outburst.

Her heart pounded as she struggled against the cuffs pinching her wrists.

The light was back in her face. She stared straight at it, even though it hurt her eyes. She refused to flinch from whomever was holding her captive.

The man laughed. "Ah, you are feisty. I can see why he wanted you."

"Who wanted me?" she asked, damned sure she knew the answer already.

"You'll see."

The light died and cast them both into darkness.

Mal braced for something horrible, not knowing what it would be or from where it might come.

A grope? A slap? A punch? A stab?

Adrenaline coursed through her body as she struggled against the cuffs. She could smell blood on her wrists as the metal dug deeper.

A knock sounded on the door.

"Ah, you have a visitor," said the man with the light.

Oh, God. He's here. He's coming to finish what he started!

Footsteps, moving away.

The door opened.

Two figures stood in silhouette against a brighter hall outside the room, both of them blurs.

Movement as the figures congregated near the door.

She kept pulling at the cuffs. Her arms were spread apart to opposite bedposts, so she couldn't reach over and dislocate her thumb to squeeze free. Mal was trapped, at the mercy of these shadowy figures.

The door closed. Silence, except the steady thrum of her heart. She froze, listening, working to determine if she were alone or if there were others in the room with her.

Others about to attack.

A light went on. She wasn't in some dungeon-like prison. The place was posh, not unlike her usual hotel room, and she wasn't alone.

A man in black was wearing a white plastic mask. He had dark skin and curly black hair. He stepped aside to reveal Jessi standing behind him, staring blankly ahead with glassy eyes. A moment of recognition, then her eyes widened.

"Detective Mallory?"

"Jessi! Oh my God, I'm so glad to see you."

She started to approach Mal, but the man beside her put a hand on her shoulder, stopping her cold.

Mal wanted to cleave that hand from his wrist.

"I'm going to uncuff you, Ms. Black. Try anything, and we'll be forced to hurt you both. Understand?"

Mal nodded, eager to say whatever might free her from the cuffs or help her to feel less vulnerable than she was when splayed on a bed.

But that wasn't the only reason. She was also looking for any chance to escape. This might be her best shot, so if an opportunity presented itself, Mal would have to act.

The man in black walked toward her.

The door eased open and a second man appeared, also in black with a white mask, He carried a pistol with a suppressor.

He raised the weapon, aiming it at the back of Jessi's head, then he leaned in, smelling strongly of a musky citrus cologne. He freed her hands, then Mal massaged throbbing red marks the metal had bitten into her wrists.

The man stepped back. "We'll bring you dinner later. We're monitoring you at all times, so don't get any ideas. Understand?"

Mal nodded.

He turned to Jessi, who also nodded.

Without another word, he left them alone. The door clicked behind him.

Jessi ran to Mal.

She took the girl into her arms, hugging her hard as they cried. "I'm soooo sorry, baby. Did they hurt you?"

"No," Jessi said, still hugging her. "But he's here."

"Who?"

"Paul Dodd."

"Did you see him?"

"They had me taking pills. I don't remember too much."

She finally pulled away, looking Mal up and down, wiping at her falling tears. "Ms. Mallory, do you know if Destinee is okay?"

"Destinee?" It took Mal a moment to place the name. "Oh, your friend on the bus?"

"Yes. The man shot her. Is she okay?"

"She's in the hospital, but she'll be okay."

"Thank God," Jessie said, sobbing harder. "I thought she was dead."

Mal hugged her again, impressed that despite Jessi's dire circumstances, her friend was top of mind.

Mal whispered, "We're going to get out of this. I promise."

"How?" she whispered back.

Mal had no idea. But she would find a way, somehow. Or perhaps Jasper would find her. "Do you know where we are?"

"Nobody's told me. I could ask someone, though."

"Who?"

"There's a girl here who has been nice. Her name is Lucia."

"She works here?"

"Yes, but I don't think she wants to."

Mal wanted to warn her not to trust other people, that not everybody is as they seem. But why rob the girl of what little innocence or hope she might have left?

Chapter 33 - Paul Dodd

"ARE YOU READY?" Madam asked as Paul was ushered into her room.

"Ready for what?"

"To open the safety deposit box."

"That depends. Where are you on my request?"

She stared at him hard, then turned on her iPad, clicked a few on-screen buttons, and turned it toward him. He saw Mallory and Jessi together on-screen, hugging and crying.

"Is everything to your satisfaction?"

Paul nodded. He wasn't sure how the hell they got Jessi, let alone Jessi *and* Mal, but they'd done it. He was impressed by their resources, and more than a little afraid. Why on earth would they keep him alive once he delivered what they wanted?

He had to secure his life. And play along until he thought of something.

"So, what happens after I get you what you want? I can't exactly go home."

"We go our separate ways. You can stay here in

Mexico, or you can go anywhere in the world. We have people to help you transition."

Paul pointed to the screen. "What about them?"

"I'm afraid they'll have to stay here in Mexico. But, if you choose to stay as well, we have a house set up, a place we use to … well, film certain movies. It has a soundproof basement. You could keep them there until you tire of them. When that happens, call me, and we'll dispose of the problem."

Just like that, *dispose of the problem.*

How long until they saw *him* as a problem? Paul was screwed. He could only smile, until he figured out a way to save himself.

"You will need this." She opened a desk drawer and retrieved a necklace with a key. "This is yours. The bank president will have the other one. And you'll need to provide the code word Wes gave you. You remember it, correct?"

"Yes," Paul lied.

Chapter 34 - Paul Dodd

THE DRIVE from Paradise to the bank was roughly twenty minutes, though it was hard to gauge time when Paul's eyes were blindfolded throughout the trip.

There were three men in the car with him, all armed, and none especially friendly.

They were his escorts. Paul couldn't stop thinking about how quickly they would put a bullet in his head the moment he recovered the drive.

The car stopped, and the man in the back with him pulled his blindfold off to reveal Banco Montaña BPI, a huge four-story building with classic Spanish architecture that made it look more like an art museum than a bank.

A man in a light blue suit approached them, smiling. He was thin, good-looking, and well dressed. "Hello, friend." He embraced Paul. "My name is Dom Diaz, and I'll be helping you navigate the language barrier with the bankers. Here is your ID." He handed Paul a wallet that was surely stuffed with copies of his documents. Why hadn't they just faked an ID and matched it to someone else's face?

"Thank you." Paul wondered how this man knew Madam Pandora.

Dom nodded to the three escorts, then they got in their car and moved it to the opposite side of the street, parking beneath a bright green awning, in a row dappled with blue, orange, and yellow buildings. People were gathered — kids hung out old men played dominoes and chess.

Paul was led into the bank, which looked surprisingly utilitarian inside compared to its impressive facade. The air was musty, like an old library or church.

Dom did most of the talking in Spanish, moving from one man to another, who looked like a manager.

He stood quietly until the manager requested his ID. He did it in English, making Paul wonder why he needed a translator. Maybe Dom wasn't a translator so much as a facilitator to ensure sure that Paul followed orders.

The man looked over his ID, then went to a computer, tapped a few keys, and invited Paul to his desk. Paul followed. He pulled out a glass pad connected to the computer and asked Paul to place his thumb on it and press.

He followed orders while the man watched his monitor, showing a thumbprint and little lines and squares superimposed as the computer attempted to match his print to the one on file.

Paul was going to ask how they had his prints, but Wes must've set it up. How *he* had the print, Paul had no idea.

The man handed him a key, then nodded, "This way, Mr. Dodd."

Dom followed as they headed toward a stairway.

The man stopped Dom and said something in Spanish.

Dom smiled, said something back in Spanish. They went back and forth until Dom nodded and offered Paul an artificial smile. He leaned over and whispered, "They

won't let me down there with you. So get the whole box and come up." Dom handed him a black cloth sack. "Drop the contents in here."

Paul took the sack and nodded, then followed the manager downstairs toward a giant vault door.

An armed guard stood outside it, barely looking at either of them as the manager opened the vault and led them inside. The room was huge, lined with safe deposit boxes from ceiling to floor. A large wooden table sat in the center. It was cold, and the vents were loud. It almost felt like a cave.

Paul wondered how many people kept their wealth and secrets hidden in the bowels of Banco Montaña BPI.

"Here you are, sir," the man said, stopping in front of a box whose metal front read 15625.

They each inserted a key, then the man pulled out the long box, and brought it to the table.

"I'll be just outside." Then he left Paul to his privacy.

Paul opened the box.

Inside was an envelope addressed to him, a flash drive, and two larger manilla envelopes.

He opened the letter.

DEAREST PAUL,

IF YOU'RE READING THIS, then things have gone terribly, terribly wrong. My only hope is that you're not caught in the web of my machinations.

You may be wondering why you're here. Perhaps you've already pieced it together. At any rate, I'm a member of a company called Voluptatem.

We're a small but powerful group of like-minded pleasure-seeking

*individuals who refuse to obey the so-called "laws" of other hypocrit-
ical men.*

*But as is the case with any group, not everybody is as discerning
as the rest. It's sad to say, but we've had to make some compromises
along the way, and some rotten apples have found their way inside.*

People with whom I cannot agree.

*I am but one voice, a single vote. I soon found my position threat-
ened by those seeking to expand this little group into something bigger,
something beyond its initial scope.*

*Seeing my days numbered, I put together enough information on
its members to secure my safety.*

That's what's in this box.

*If they are responsible for my passing, I hope you will use the
flash drive to burn them.*

*If not, and I've died by natural causes, then allow this to serve as
your membership into said group. Maybe you can make it into something better than we ever managed.*

*There is an encrypted flash drive in the box. The key is the name
of the book I gave you. No spaces.*

PAUL THOUGHT FOR A MOMENT, then remembered looking
at Wes's bookshelf and seeing a book that caught his interest. Hitler's *Mein Kampf.*

He had heard of it and wondered what could possibly
be inside. Paul wasn't a racist, nor did he have any opinion
on Jews. But the book had a forbidden air, and thus made
him curious.

Wes handed it over. Sadly, the book was nowhere near
as interesting as Paul had imagined, and he never even
finished reading it.

. . .

I'VE SET up a website with a password protected page, built on blockchain. Once you've opened this box, the bank president was instructed to make the website live. It's programmed to require your typing the book title, all caps, no spaces, into a box on the thirtieth of every month. If you fail, the information will be unencrypted and sent to the press.

This is my poison pill to ensure your safety. Tell Madam Pandora about this website, without revealing the URL, and you will be safe.

Lastly, I want to apologize to both you and your sister. I hope you can find it in your hearts to one day forgive me.

Love,

Wes

PAUL WIPED the tears from his eyes then took the contents of the box.

Chapter 35 - Jessi Price

JESSI WAITED on the bed as Miss Mallory showered.

It felt good to have someone else here with her, even though she knew Mallory was taken against her will, too, and was scared. She tried to act like she was fine, but Jessi wasn't dumb.

Jessi was also scared, but with Mallory here, she had to be brave. Maybe if they were both strong enough they could figure a way out of this place.

They'd done it before, after all. And while the memories were still fuzzy, Jessi remembered feeling hopeless then, too.

But now there was more than just Paul. There were a bunch of people in some weird hotel or something, keeping them prisoner. How did Lucia fit into it all? She seemed like a good person, even if she was working with the bad guys. Jessi wasn't sure how Lucia could help them, especially if she was a prisoner, too.

Mallory came out of the bathroom dressed in jeans and a T-shirt. It looked a lot more comfortable than the dress.

Jessi wished she could get some more comfortable clothes, but they'd only given her dresses that made her feel like a doll. She wondered if these people knew any real girls her age. Why would they think a girl would *only* want to wear dresses?

"Did I miss anything?" Miss Mallory asked.

"Nobody's been here. But I think dinner is soon. Are you hungry?"

"Yeah. Have they been feeding you three meals a day?"

"Yes. Most of the people have been nice, except for making me take medicine. What is this place?"

Mallory paused. "Truthfully, I don't know. I've never seen a place like this. You've only been in your room, right?"

"Right."

"And you didn't see anyone else?"

"Only the ones I told you about."

"Any idea how big the place is? Or how many people there are?"

"No. Sorry."

"Who usually brings you food?"

"Lucia. Though there's always a man with her, and he has a gun."

"The same man or different ones?"

"Different."

"How many different ones."

"Um, maybe three?"

"And do you see the same ones at the same times? Like the same guy in the morning each day, then a different guy at noon, and so on?"

Jessi thought, but some of her days were still fuzzy. "I can't really remember. I think it's been different people all day. Like one guy all day and then another the next."

"But Lucia always comes?"

"Yes, she's been there each time."

Mallory was quiet, thinking. Jessi didn't want to interrupt her by asking why she was asking so many specifics. Even though they kept their voices low, Mallory had warned Jessi that the people might hear them.

A woman's voice came over the speaker. "It's dinner time. Sit on the bed and do not do anything stupid. Do you understand?"

Mallory and Jessi both said yes. Mallory sat on the bed beside Jessi.

The door opened.

Lucia entered, rolling a cart with covered plates and drinks.

The door stayed open, and standing guard just inside was one of the men in black, a heavy guy with a big bushy beard, holding a gun.

Lucia smiled. "How are you today, Jessi?"

"Okay. This is Mallory."

"Hello," Lucia said, meeting Mallory's eyes before quickly turning back to the food.

"Can I ask you a question?"

Lucia looked to the guard, staring at them blankly, then back at Mallory. "Sure."

"Why are we here?"

"I don't know. They don't tell me."

"What *do* they tell you?"

"They tell me to keep our guests happy, and that's what I try to do."

Mallory sounded mean, but Jessi didn't want to say anything that might upset her or cause a scene. She'd hate it if Lucia stopped coming.

Lucia raised the covers to reveal chicken, rice, and veggies, steam pluming off of the plates, the smell rumbling Jessi's stomach.

"How old are you?" Mallory asked.

"Seventeen."

"What is this place?"

"Paraíso," Lucia said, handing a plate to Jessi.

"What is *Paraíso?*"

"An exclusive destination for guests with discriminating tastes," Lucia said, handing the second plate to Mallory.

"And that's what we are? *Guests?* We didn't ask to be here. We were kidnapped."

"Ma'am, I don't know—"

The voice boomed over the speaker. "Please, Ms. Black, be quiet and let Lucia do her job."

"I just want some answers!"

"You will get them soon enough. For now, please enjoy your meal and your visit. We're trying to be as accommodating as possible given the circumstances. Don't force us to be … *less accommodating.*"

Lucia handed Mallory a bottle of water and whispered, "Don't upset them." Her eyes were urgent, bordering on terror. "Please." She handed a second bottle to Jessi.

Mallory shut her mouth and watched Lucia rolled the cart out of their room. The guard followed, then locked the door behind them.

"Sorry," Mallory said, though she wasn't sure if she was apologizing to Jessi or whoever was watching.

Jessi pressed her fork into the rice. It hit something that wasn't food.

She kept eating, slowly uncovering what was stuck inside the rice so that the camera wouldn't catch her. She saw a rolled-up piece of white paper, covered in rice, so she put it in her mouth, then excused herself to the restroom.

She hoped there weren't cameras in the bathroom, but Jessi couldn't be sure, so she put her hand on her stomach

and made a terrible grimace before falling to her knees and coughing into her hand.

The piece of paper, along with clumps of wet rice, dropped into her palm. She kept retching, pushing her hair back from the toilet.

"Are you okay?" Mallory asked from outside the door.

"Just feeling a little pukey," Jessi said, trying to look and sound as authentically sick as possible for whomever might be listening.

She resumed her position hunched over the toilet, hand hidden in her hair, unrolling the piece of paper. Once unfolded, she went back to gagging, her face practically in the bowl as she bought herself seconds of reading time.

I will find a way to help you. Just be patient.

Tears stung her eyes, touched that this girl who didn't even know her would risk everything to help.

Jessi flushed the paper along with the stuff she'd spit into the toilet.

Be patient.

She had to find a way to let Mallory know, so she wouldn't do anything to anger their captors or prevent Lucia from helping.

Chapter 36 - Paul Dodd

DANIEL USHERED Paul into Madam Pandora's room then promptly left.

Paul, holding the black cloth bag with the contents of the box, took a seat opposite her desk.

The way she stared at him without any emotion chilled him to the marrow. This was a woman who couldn't care less if he lived or died. He'd had that look from many women, including his ex-wife, but those stares were different. They didn't belong to someone with the power to make his immediate death a distinct possibility.

"You have the flash drive?" This sounded less like an inquiry than a command.

"Yes." Paul reached into the bag and handed the drive right over.

"And what else was in the box?"

"Photos, of a rather disturbing nature."

"I would like those as well."

He pulled out the envelope and slid it across the desk.

"Anything else?"

He wondered if she knew. Maybe she was testing his leverage.

A new fear crept into his skull. What if this was all a test to see if he could be trusted? What if the moment he tried to blackmail her — only to assure his safety, but blackmail no less — they decided that he wasn't worthy of membership in their club? Then of course they would kill him.

He'd been dreading this moment when he thought it was the right thing. Now, self-doubt riddled his every thought. If this was a test, then Paul was about to fail.

"There was cash and some bearer bonds."

"Those are yours to do with as you wish. Though once you leave our protection, I would advise you put them back in the bank. I'm sure you're aware of the danger of carrying those around."

"Yes," he said, surprised she was giving him advice as if she cared about his welfare. Maybe he shouldn't say anything about the back-up plan. Maybe he should keep his mouth shut, be grateful, leave the room, then get on with his new life.

But the iciness in Pandora's eyes reminded him to trust his gut, and his instincts said Wes was right not to trust these people. "There is one other thing."

She folded her hands on the desk. "Yes?"

His heart throbbed in his neck as he worked up the courage to lay it all on the line. "There is a digital copy of the flash drive connected to a website that Wes set up."

"What?" She leaned forward ever so slightly, her hands still folded.

"It's programmed to send the documents to several agencies and media outlets if anything should happen to me, or if I don't give it weekly instructions to stand down."

"This is unacceptable. What if something happens to you? What if you should, let's say, die from natural causes? Then you're going to blow up Paraíso?"

"I have precautions in place. And we can work out those details after I'm safe. No offense, Madam, but Wes advised me to protect myself. He said there were people on the board that couldn't be trusted."

"Oh, really? And which people might that be?"

Paul smiled, trying to convey a confidence he wasn't particularly feeling. "I can't betray a dead man's trust."

"But you will betray *us*?"

"No. I'll keep my mouth shut like a good little boy. But, you have to admit, I'm in a precarious situation, a fugitive wanted for murder in a country where I don't know anyone, and I've recently inherited a sizable fortune. I think you can appreciate that I'd want to assure my safety."

"The board won't be pleased."

"I've given that some thought. And I'm willing to surrender my shares so that our interests are more aligned."

"Your shares? Do you realize the value and power you'd be giving up?"

"I don't need either. I just want to live the rest of my life free from worry, the law, and business partners stabbing me in the back."

"I'm not sure the board will be happy to know that this digital suicide pill exists."

"Then don't tell them. All I need is for you to assure my safety. Can you do that?"

She stared at Paul as a cold silence settled over him, his every fiber ordering him to apologize and get the hell out of there before Pandora ordered him dead.

She nodded, barely moving. "You have a deal, Mr. Dodd."

Madam offered her hand and they shook, though Paul would wait until he was out of the room to finally exhale.

Chapter 37 - Paul Dodd

AFTER FINALIZING the details of their arrangement, Paul was free to wander Paradise as a full-fledged member while Madam Pandora put the final touches on his new home.

Inside the elevator, Daniel turned to him before pressing any buttons. "Where would you like to go, sir?"

"What are my options?"

"We have two different clubs. A dance club and a gentleman's club. We also have several bars including one outdoor at the pool. Also, a world class restaurant that—"

"A pool bar? Yes, I'd like to go there."

Daniel pressed the rooftop button and they began their ascent.

"Shall I get you some clothing more appropriate for swimming?"

"Yes, I'd like that. Thank you."

Paul wondered if he'd made a mistake by surrendering his seat on the board. He could get used to this sort of treatment, and the kind of benefits that Paradise provided. Spoiled, even.

The elevator doors dinged open to a bright rooftop

pool and bar, a DJ blasting Europop, and a mix of wealthy but mostly ugly men and stunning models ranging from mid-teen to early thirties. The pool ran into a grotto where Paul imagined people were fucking as if it were the Playboy Mansion.

Daniel led him past a row of lounge chairs toward the bar. Paul scanned the area, searching for younger children. He didn't see any yet.

He wondered if this is where they kept things more legit. It was on a rather high mountain rooftop with no buildings looking directly down onto it, but Paul imagined the authorities or other busy bodies could use drones to surveil the area. Best to keep the illegal shit away from prying eyes.

Daniel introduced him to a beautiful caramel-skinned blonde with piercing blue eyes. "Maria, this is Mr. Paul. Take good care of him, will you?"

"Hello. What can I get for you, Mr. Paul?" She flashed a killer smile. Perfect cleavage spilled out from her tight yellow bikini.

"Surprise me," he said, feeling adventurous.

"That's the spirit, sir!" Daniel slapped Paul on the back. "I'll be back shortly, with a change of clothing."

Moments later, Maria returned with a drink. "Here you go, Mr. Paul. A Pancho Villa."

He didn't ask what it was. He simply raised the glass to his lips and sucked it down.

A short while later, Paul was lying on a lounge chair wearing shorts, a red tee, and shades. The sun kissed his skin, making him wish he wasn't so damned self-conscious about the scars on his back. It seemed, particularly in a place like this where women were paid, or forced, to be kind, that nobody would freak out. But there was no disguising their eyes. And, for now, he wanted to enjoy the

proclivities. Maybe she'd done the math or had information on him that he wasn't aware of.

"What's your name?" the girl asked.

"Paul."

"Paul," she repeated in her raspy voice.

Another model came over carrying a tray of colorful shots. "Jell-O?" she said in a thick Spanish accent.

"No, thank you." Paul didn't want to dull his senses, not with this beautiful creature sitting with him.

"Two blues," Sally said.

Paul was surprised. Wondered if he should say something.

The woman handed them over and left. Sally lifted one to her lips and let the jiggly blue treat tumble into her tiny mouth.

"You like those?" he asked, only now noticing the girl's glassy eyes.

"*Sí*. I mean, yes." Sally laughed. "You want?" She thrust the other shot glass to his mouth playfully.

He opened his mouth and she poured it inside. It was sweet, but strong.

She laughed as some of it spilled from his mouth. She moved in, so fast he didn't even know what she was doing, and licked the Jell-O from his chin.

Her body was pressed against his, her wet bathing suit soaking his shirt and shorts.

She threw her arms around him and slid her tongue into his mouth.

Paul was shocked, his first instinct was to push her away before someone saw, but his brain didn't tell his hands, and he let her.

And then he remembered where he was.

He kissed her back, his tongue darting around in her

mouth. It was weird to be kissing someone with such little experience. And arousing as hell.

She laughed and pulled away, smiling mischievously. "You a good kisser."

"Thank you." His face flushed.

She kissed him again, and then met his eyes. He thought about the fear in all the other girls' eyes, the fear that had ruined the illusion that they wanted him. This girl shower no fear, only a sly smile. She seemed to actually want him.

"Go back to your room?" she asked.

"God, yes."

Chapter 38 - Mallory Black

Mal woke up in her bed at home with Ashley cuddled up against her.

Her stuffed teddy bear, Pinky, was crammed awkwardly between them, looking up at Mal in the soft blue glow of her alarm clock as if to say, "Help, I can't breathe!"

Mal gently pulled Pinky out from between them and set her on top of Ashley's back.

Sometimes Mal would go in before Ashley woke up and set Pinky up in some amusing way — sitting on her nightstand "reading" a book; hanging from her doorknob; or propped up on the ground in front of her closet, on the back of the toilet, or inside the shower.

Mal looked at her daughter, admiring how sweet she looked when sleeping. She was ten and growing too fast, but sometimes she still looked so much like a little girl.

Mal flashed back to the countless times Ashley had fallen asleep on her as a baby and toddler, and how many times she'd watched her eyes flutter behind their lids, wondering what she might be dreaming.

When Ashley was old enough to talk, Mal would some-

times ask her what she'd dreamed about, but she never seemed to remember.

Ashley's feet kicked out and she flinched, her face finding a frightened expression.

Mal sat up, watching her with concern, wanting to reach out and gently wake her, to ease her out of the nightmare. She touched her shoulder, and Ashley's eyes shot open.

She screamed, "You should have killed him!"

And just like that, Ashley's flesh began to fall away, rotting like a pumpkin caving in on itself.

Mal cried out, scared and confused, "Ashley! What's happening?"

She reached out to push the girl's skin back onto her face, but it was too late.

Teeth were falling from her skull.

Eyes burrowed out, dark holes of rot, right into her brain.

Mal screamed.

Then she woke to find Jessi in her arms. She remembered, again, that her daughter was dead. And then, where she was.

Jessi looked at her with wide, frightened eyes. "What's wrong?"

Their door burst open and four men in black stormed inside, two with guns, and the others with needles. One of the men said, "Time to go!"

Mal wasn't sure where they were going, nor did she care. She panicked, seeing what might be their last shot at escaping this place, and launched herself toward the nearest man. She reached for his gun, but someone hit her hard in the back of the head.

Mal collapsed to the ground, pain exploding in her skull.

"Shouldn't have done that." He pressed a rifle to her temple.

Jessi screamed, "Mallory!" and dove toward her.

One of the men grabbed Jessi by the hair and yanked her backward. She screamed and the man stuck a needle in Jessi.

Then the other one pierced Mal's neck.

Chapter 39 - Jasper Parish

EVEN THOUGH HE made Anders drive the entire twenty-something hours to Texas, then kept him behind the wheel while crossing the border, Jasper was still exhausted.

But there was no time to rest now as they entered the city of El Barranco.

Anders had been quiet through most of the drive. A few times, he'd tried to beg for his family's release, then plead his case — he wasn't a bad guy, Jasper had no idea how powerful these people were, forcing him to do their bidding as they were.

"You kidnapped a kid and a cop," Jasper said every time. "There's no way you come out looking like the good guy here."

"Yeah, but you kidnapped my wife and daughter. So what does that make *you*?"

"I've no illusions that I'm some angel. Way I see it, the world needs a few devils to keep the truly wicked from running the show."

Jasper didn't push the argument far, mostly keeping

Anders talking about BlackBriar to determine how deep the guilt ran.

According to Anders, he organized everything. Victor didn't know dick.

Jasper found it hard to believe but needed the man to think he might make it out of this weekend alive. He was no good if he realized the depths of his troubles.

Earlier, Anders had tried to avoid telling Jasper too much, saying that he was putting his life, and his family's lives, at risk. But Jasper convinced him that when this was all done, he'd help him get out from under the thumb of these hidden puppeteers. Jasper tried to get some names, people who were pulling the strings, but Anders claimed to know nothing. Most interactions were done via anonymous Internet chat. They'd found some dirt and got him to comply by threatening his ruin.

"I tried to get out a few times, and then they did what you did — terrorized my family. It's hard to do the right thing when you've got someone threatening to rape and murder your six-year-old child."

If his story was true, Jasper felt bad. Still, he had no intention of letting the man live beyond his usefulness.

Anders merged off the main road and began a slow ascent up a winding mountain road.

"This is it, at the top. Paraíso, or Paradise." Anders nodded at the large hotel's meandering roofline. "It's got everything you could want — gambling, women, fine dining, and nightly entertainment."

Jasper made him go over their story again. Anders was bringing a big fish, Jasper going by the name Reginald Oliver, as his guest for a weekend of depravity. They would indulge in food, drinks, and women until they were full.

Once inside, Anders would get Jasper an audience with

the woman who ran the operation, then Jasper would find and free Jessi and Mallory. After that, Dodd was dead.

Anders said Madam Pandora was a smart business woman and enough money could get her to betray their pedophile guest. He hoped it would go down that easily. If it didn't, he'd have to improvise. And he'd be more or less going up against a small army of guards and whatever corrupt police Madam had on her payroll. It could get ugly, quick. Jasper hoped Anders loved his family enough to keep things running smoothly.

They arrived at a gatehouse where Anders showed a card to the armed guard. The heavy black iron gates slowly opened, allowing their entry onto the compound.

The isolated mountain resort was a sprawling four story building with sleek architecture and old-world aesthetics. It would have looked like any other five-star hotel, if not for the armed men situated at key points of entry, looking out along the long roof.

Jasper felt the odds of an armed escape melting to nothing as they drove deeper into the lion's den.

They parked on the first floor parking garage, then got out, grabbed their suitcases from the trunk, and walked to an elevator leading to an ornate entrance with high wood-beamed ceilings and lush red carpets.

Anders led them to the reception desk where he checked them into one of the suites.

A bellhop came up with a cart and offered to take their luggage. Anders nodded.

As the man loaded their suitcases, Jasper hoped he wouldn't notice the weight, or worse, call security to check them. Jasper had come well-equipped for battle, with rifles, pistols, ammunition, knives, grenades, and a gas mask.

The bellhop loaded the bags then led them toward the elevators, dragging the cart behind them all the way to

their third floor suite. Anders tipped the man after he unloaded the suitcases into their room. With the bellhop gone and the room their own, Jasper opened one of his bags and grabbed his hidden camera and microphone detector. Then he swept the room, searching for Wi-Fi or infrared signals.

Once he was sure that they weren't being watched, Jasper retrieved a pistol and two knives then slipped them into a discreet jacket holster.

Anders stared at him. "You going to give me one?"

"That depends, are you going to shoot me in the back?"

"Maybe after I get my family back."

Jasper handed him a Beretta and suppressor. "You don't use it unless shit goes south."

Anders looked at him like he was an idiot. "You forget my extensive training or time with the SEALs?"

"I'm just making sure we're on the same page, the one where we all get out of this alive — you, me, Jessi Price, Mallory Black, and, of course, your family."

"No need to remind me." Anders glared at him.

Jasper wondered how much the man was already plotting against him. He was probably mentally hiring a sketch artist to draw Jasper then run him through some recognition program to discover his identity. The moment Anders got his family back safely, there was no stone he'd leave unturned in pursuit of revenge. Even if Jasper wanted to keep Anders alive, it was just too big a risk.

Anders made a call and asked if he could meet with Madam Pandora, saying he wanted to introduce her to someone very important. He nodded as the person on the other end of the phone replied, then sighed. "Okay. We'll be waiting."

"She's tied up at the moment. So we have a couple of

hours to kill. You mind if we get something to eat? I'm starving. And you should at least try the food here before you get us kicked out permanently."

Jasper nodded. "Fine."

They freshened up then took the elevator downstairs to 1862, presumably named after Mexico's victory over French invaders.

The restaurant was surrounded by windows, show-casing spectacular views of the mountains rolling around them. The ceilings were high, the wood polished and dark. Jasper and Anders sat at a table in the rear, Jasper with his back to the wall, same way he always sat whenever he went anywhere, much less deep into enemy territory.

Jasper ordered Carne Asada a la Tampiqueña, with hand mashed guacamole, rajas, black beans and Calabac-itas Rellenas, plus a Pancho Villa, the house specialty.

As he waited for their food, Jasper surveyed the restau-rant, noticing how many men were there with beautiful women well out of their league. While he was used to seeing this arrangement in finer restaurants and clubs, there were quite a few very young women with much older men, including several girls as young as twelve or thirteen, made up like women twice their age, in nice dresses and jewelry.

An obese, balding man sat in a corner booth, wearing a bad suit and oversized shades. He was on his cell phone shouting about some actor being difficult on his set and how he wished he'd never hired him. Typical Hollywood douchebag if not for his date, a blonde Russian-looking girl that couldn't have been more than fourteen, sitting next to him with glazed eyes, barely touching her chocolate cake.

Hollywood Douchebag hung up the phone and turned back to the girl, saying something Jasper couldn't hear as the man pulled her toward him. She smiled awkwardly as

he picked up her fork and fed her dessert. Then he grabbed her hand and put in his lap.

Jasper wanted to get up and feed the man the fork, straight into his neck.

Their waiter arrived with their meals, plated exquisitely with an eye for presentation that you'd typically find only in a Michelin restaurant.

As Jasper watched Hollywood and the girl, his appetite faded. All he could see in the place were dirty old men with little girls. He wondered how many were here against their will versus by some other circumstance. Any answer would make him sick.

He wanted to get up and put a bullet in each of these pervert's heads.

Instead, he took a long drink of wine to calm himself.

Anders, digging into his food, looked at him. "You okay?"

"How can you just sit here and eat with all this shit going on?"

Anders smiled. "You haven't seen the worst of it. The club or the grotto will get your blood boiling."

"And these are the people you work for? How, with these women and girls being exploited?"

Anders kept eating, calmer than anyone should be in a place like this. "How's the view from up there in your ivory tower?"

"Fuck you."

"I'm not being flip. I'm being serious. Many of these girls are from third-world shit holes. Here they have a chance to earn money and send it back to their families so they don't live in abject poverty."

Jasper snorted. "Please. I'm familiar with the slave industry. Most of these girls are taken against their will.

Forced to do horrible shit, not making any money except for their pimps."

"You watch too many movies, *Reginald*. Hell, half their families don't even want them. They sell them. What chance did they ever have? Why not get some use out of them while they're still of value?"

"You wouldn't be saying that if it was your daughter here."

"You act like they've got it awful. But look around. This place is heaven. These girls are cared for, get medical help, and they make some money. They have more opportunities here than they would back home where they weren't even wanted."

"That what you tell yourself so you can sleep at night?" Jasper took another sip to stem his rage. The more Anders spoke, the more Jasper was convinced his participation wasn't coercion so much as a witting, willing participant in this dark and terrible business.

Jasper went to set his glass on the table but knocked it over instead. He went to grab it, but missed, spilling his Pancho Villa on the table and onto his lap. He tried to move out of the way, but suddenly everything was moving in slow motion.

Anders said, "That would be the drugs taking effect."

Jasper reached for his gun, but instead he fell to the floor.

Chapter 40 - Jasper Parish

JASPER WOKE to a slap in the face.

He looked around and as he got his bearings, realized he was naked, sitting in a chair in a dark room, hands restrained behind him. He could hear, and feel, loud electronic music and bass coming from not too far away.

He got an immediate sense of *déjà vu*.

Bright light burned above him. The floor was concrete, the walls and ceilings unfinished. It felt like a basement. Maybe under the club.

Footsteps behind him, felt more than heard above the music.

"You're awake."

Anders stepped into view. "Who are you?"

"You want your wife and daughter to die?"

Anders smiled. "Funny thing, that. You see, I have people watching them all the time. I knew it wouldn't be long before they went into action."

"Bullshit."

Anders reached into his pocket, pulled out his phone,

flipped through a few screens, then showed his wife and daughter smiling in a room, standing next to some big guy.

"See, they're okay." He pulled the phone back, scrolled a bit, then showed Jasper a photo of two dead black men, gunshots to their heads, execution style. "Though I can't say the same for your guys."

Jasper's heart plummeted into his gut.

He wondered how far up the ladder they followed the lead. If they'd gotten to Spider. He hated to think he'd gotten a good kid like that killed.

"So," Anders said, "again, who are you?"

"Nobody."

Anders laughed, then smacked Jasper hard in the face. "Wrong answer. You are going to tell me who the hell you are, who you work for, and everything else I want to know."

Jasper said nothing, smiling up at his tormentor.

"We've got your phone. It won't take us long to decrypt it, find all your contacts, and get the info. We'll find those closest to you and kill them all once we do."

Jasper doubted they'd get past his encryption, but even if they did, he'd deleted most of the contact info for anyone close to him. Though, that number was small these days — really only Alicia.

Still, there were associates, including Spider, and if they hadn't already gotten to her, then they might be able to do it with the info on his phone.

But that wasn't his biggest concern. No, that was escaping, finding Jessi and Mallory, then getting the hell out of this place — which would be significantly harder to do without his weapons or Anders' help.

"A guy like you isn't a freelancer, no. You FBI?"

"Yeah, and if you do anything to me, you're in for a

world of hurt. You think your family is safe, but I got people, too."

A door opened behind Anders and a short Spanish woman entered wearing a black dress that matched her jet-black hair. Behind her was a tall, muscular, bald man holding a machete.

Jasper remembered his nightmare, and the world of hurt he was in for.

The woman, surely Madam Pandora, said, "Why did you come here?"

"To save Jessi Price and Mallory Black."

"Why?" The woman circled around him, looking him up and down.

"Because I don't want them to die," Jasper said, wondering what kind of question was that — *why?*

"Who are they to you?"

Jasper looked past her and toward the brute in the corner, waiting to put his blade to use. He wondered how many others had been dragged down to this basement and butchered. How many cops, politicians, and, of course, girls who disobeyed them?

"I asked you a question," she calmly repeated, stopping in front of him and looking down at his naked body with a smirk.

Jasper had never felt more vulnerable, but he refused to give either Madam or Anders the satisfaction of any emotion beyond a cold, hard stare.

"I told your man, I work with the FBI."

"No, you don't. You're not in any database. We've looked. So, again, who are you?"

"Someone who can pay you incredibly well to free them."

"What is incredibly well?"

"You name the price," Jasper said. "I can get my hands on it."

She stared into his eyes. "Any price?"

"Any price."

"Fifteen million."

"Not a problem."

"Each."

"Again, not a problem."

"Bullshit," Anders said, "I say we kill him."

"Seriously. I can get you thirty million, easily. Just let me make a few calls."

Anders looked like he was going to object, but Madam Pandora raised a finger to silence him.

She leaned over and got right in front of Jasper, inches from his face. He could smell her sweet perfume. Could see her pulse quickening along her neck.

She was considering his offer.

"I think you *could* get me the money. Which makes me even more curious who you are."

"Let them go, then I'll tell you. And I'll pay you."

"I'm sorry, Mister … whatever your name is. I run a place of discretion and trust. If I sell out one of my own clients to a higher bidder, what would that tell my other clients?"

"Nobody needs to know." Jasper's voice cracked as he pled. It was too close to begging, and that made him feel weak. "Just let them go. They don't need to die."

She went to the brute. "I want his name." Then she turned to Anders. "Come, Mr. Martin. We've things to discuss."

"Please," Jasper called out, but Madam Pandora ignored his plea.

The door closed.

But only for a moment. Then it opened and another pair of men entered. Not as large, but equally menacing.

The first man looked Jasper up and down. "I don't suppose you're going to give me a name?"

Jasper shook his head.

Chapter 41 - Mallory Black

MAL WOKE to jostling in darkness, the world around her nothing but hums and vibrations, the stench of gasoline as the van drove over an unpaved road.

Her hands were cuffed behind her. The van was too dark to see, so she whispered, "Jessi?"

No response.

She rolled over, slowly, and bumped into someone. She prayed it wasn't a corpse, especially Jessi's. She moved closer.

"Jessi?"

Still nothing.

Mal felt with her cheek and her head, pressing against the body until she confirmed that it was most likely Jessi beside her. She brought her head to the girl's chest, listened for a heartbeat, and sighed with relief when she felt and heard it.

Still alive ... for now.

The van continued bumping along the road as Mal evaluated her situation. Their captors were taking them somewhere, but where? She wasn't sure how long she'd

been out, or how long they'd been driving. Most confusing of all was *why* they were being moved.

They had been in a secure place with armed men. Why move them?

Because, she knew in her heart, they were being disposed of. Which meant the next time that door opened, Mal needed to find a way to kill whatever motherfucker was in front of her.

Kill them, break free, and escape before more bad guys came.

Easy, right?

Her police academy training had never prepared her for this scenario, or anything like it. But it had taught Mal that you never let your captors take you anywhere. Once abducted and moved from one location to another, the odds of survival practically disappeared.

So with the odds not on their side, they needed fate to intervene.

But how likely was that, twice in their lives?

Again she thought of Parish, who might very well be their only hope. If he was truly psychic, had he seen this happening? She thought back to their phone call and his warning — they'd be with Dodd again and not to stop him.

Did she dare to hope his prediction played out? If so, then this wasn't the end quite yet.

But it was hard to trust anything Jasper said. He was clearly missing some cards from his deck. He thought his dead daughter was alive. How the hell could she trust a word he said?

He knew Ashley was in danger. And that both you and Jessi were in danger, twice.

The man might be crazy, but he clearly knew *something*.

Still, Mal couldn't count on him being right this time.

If she saw an opportunity, she needed to strike. To take fate into her own hands and find a way out of this jam.

A siren blurted behind the van. Twice.

She sat up, her heart racing as fate seemed to be intervening yet again.

Did she dare to hope against hope?

The van pulled over.

Yes!

She heard two men in the front of the van saying something in Spanish, one of them clearly trying to calm the other down.

Then she heard footsteps approaching the rear of the van.

Yes! Yes!

Now was the time.

She kicked at the floor and screamed, "Help! Help!"

The cop's voice boomed, demanding something of the driver.

More back-and-forth in Spanish. She couldn't understand the words, but had heard some variation of the conversation, or had it herself, hundreds of times before.

Hands up and let me search your vehicle.

"Help me!" She screamed so loud, nobody could mistake her panic.

Footsteps came around to the rear.

The doors opened, daylight spilling in before giving way to the police officer standing there with whom she assumed to be her driver and his accomplice.

The police officer looked at her.

"Please, help me!" Mal cried out trying to crawl toward him. "These men kidnapped us."

She looked down to see Jessi, still passed out, hands cuffed behind her.

The cop looked at the two men then said something in Spanish.

This is it. He's going to arrest them, and we're free.

But that wasn't happening.

Instead one of the two men grabbed a rag from his pocket, climbed into the van, and shoved the rag into Mal's mouth — while the cop stood there.

What the fuck?

Mal head butted the man hard and scrambled toward the open doors.

The cop pulled his gun on her and yelled, "Stop!"

Mal froze, realizing what was happening. "You motherfucker."

The man she'd head butted slammed her head against the side of the van and spit out, "Puta!" before climbing out of the van.

The doors closed again.

And Mal screamed through the rag in her mouth.

Chapter 42 - Jasper Parish

Jasper woke alone in a dark room, hands tied behind him, sitting in a chair, a bright light burning into his eyes. Everything was fuzzy. His vision,' and how he'd gotten here.

Dad!

He tilted his head, thinking he'd heard something, but the only thing reaching his ears was the dull thrumming of music coming from nearby. He must be in a room under the club.

Every part of his body ached. He'd been battered, cut, and water boarded to within an inch of his life, the men holding him wanting him to "just fucking tell them."

What they wanted him to say, he wasn't sure. It was all vague.

"Dad!" he heard a girl's voice in the distance, as if underwater.

No, not a girl, but his daughter, Jordyn. "Dad!"

He looked around, his vision fuzzy, blood seeping from his brow into his eyes, hot, stinging and sticky. But Jasper couldn't see her.

He heard movement behind him, turned his head. But it wasn't Jordyn. It was a big bald man, the first of his attackers, dragging a machete against the ground. "You ready to tell us?"

"Dad! Remember!"

Jasper had a flash of his vision, and what had happened before, how it had ended so horribly.

He had brought it on himself, and remembered exactly what happened with a sudden, terrible clarity.

The hulking man stared down at him, glaring.

After hours of torture, Jasper had given him nothing, and now the man was sick of his bullshit, was within a hair's breadth of snapping and doing what brutes like him did best — getting stupidly violent. The man's grip tightened on the blade, itching to swing it. All he needed was one little push.

Jasper leaned slightly forward in the chair, hands still bound by something tight. It wasn't cuffs, which meant he could eventually break free.

He whispered something to draw the man forward, just a bit more.

"What was that?"

Jasper laughed.

The man's eyes bulged.

Then Jasper gave him the push he needed. "Fuck you."

The man snapped, then came at Jasper, swinging the machete.

But Jasper had seen the man's move in his vision, and easily moved to counter it.

He pushed himself up from the chair with every molecule of his remaining strength, before the man could bring the machete down.

Jasper's forehead slammed into the man's face with a sickening crunch.

The guy stumbled back, blood flowing from his broken nose.

Jasper raised his foot and kicked him hard, right in the chest. Then he pushed his wrists together, raised his arms over the small of his back, and brought them down, breaking the zip tie.

As Jasper righted himself, the brute was coming at him, screaming, machete raised.

Jasper looked up just in time to sidestep him, swiftly sweeping his foot out and causing the big man to tumble forward straight into the chair.

He dropped the machete in an attempt to save himself from a face plant.

Jasper scrambled toward the machete and grabbed the handle.

The brute had tumbled over the chair, breaking it on impact, but was already getting back up.

Jasper raced toward him then thrust the blade through his gut.

The brute cried out as the blade sliced through his stomach and out his back.

His eyes were wide, his face sported a painful scowl. Hot sticky blood poured onto Jasper's hands as he gripped the blade tight and twisted it upward, doing as much damage as possible before yanking it free and letting the man fall back to the ground, twitching and gasping.

Jasper plunged the blade through the man's temple, into his brain, to make sure he wasn't just dead, but quiet. Then he sighed while searching for his clothes.

He found them sitting in a pile behind him.

"Quick, Dad!" Jordyn said, now in the room. "Before they come with their guns."

Jasper craned his neck to listen but didn't hear anyone coming just yet. He hoped the music was loud enough to mask his kill.

He threw on his clothes and shoes, disappointed that his gun and knives weren't in the pile. At least he had the machete.

Jordyn placed her palm flat against the door and said, "There's one guard in the hall."

"That's it?"

"Yeah. He's ten feet away, facing the other way."

Jasper approached the door, adjusting his grip on the sticky handle, then opened the door.

The music was louder in the hall, enough to easily mask Jasper's footsteps.

The guard, one of the men who had been in the torture room earlier, was at the end of the hall, looking down at his cell phone, facing the other way, an AR-15 dangling from his shoulder by the strap.

Jasper crept up behind him.

At the last moment, whether he'd heard Jasper or felt him, the man spun around.

His eyes widened he dropped the phone and tried to raise the rifle and squeeze off a shot. But Jasper sunk the machete's blade straight down the center of the man's skull before he could, dropping him to the ground.

Jasper left the blade in his skull, then yanked the rifle from the man's corpse, a process made more difficult by the rifle sling wrapped around the lifeless body.

He pulled the AR-15 free, wiped the handle, then did a press check and peered inside the chamber to make sure a round wasn't already in there.

Nope.

He pulled the charging bolt back, then let it go, pulling a round into the chamber.

Jasper selected SEMI on his selector switch and checked the extended magazine, which was full.

A suppressor on the rifle added to the rifle's weight, and he'd need to adjust his shot, but it was better to avoid drawing too much attention, assuming the bullets were subsonic. Otherwise, the shots might still be loud, suppressor be damned. Thankfully the weapon didn't have any shitty extra optics.

He slowly ascended the stairs. As he went up, he saw a shadow moving, growing larger on the wall.

The other man?

Jasper raced up the stairs, saw the other guy in the upstairs hall, holding a drink and not paying attention. He took aim and said, "Put the gun down."

Jasper was afraid that the man didn't speak English, but he obeyed, placing his rifle on the ground while staring at his assailant with wide eyes. Probably frightened by the blood on Jasper's suit and face.

"Where is Madam?"

The man pointed up.

"What floor is she on?"

"Fourth."

"Kick the gun over."

He did.

Jasper bent down, removed the cartridge and slipped it into his jacket pocket. "You got any more guns?"

The man reached into his jacket.

"Slow!"

He slowed down, reached inside his jacket, grabbed the pistol, then lowered it to the ground and kicked it over.

Jasper picked it up and slipped it into his back waistband. "You're gonna take me to see Madam."

The man nodded.

Jasper removed his jacket, threw it over the top of the AR-15, then put the pistol against his back. "Walk."

Jasper followed the man, keeping him close so anyone who happened to see them wouldn't take notice of what was happening. They walked through the door and into the club, a cavernous space, dark and packed with people.

The techno was loud. Colorful lights on and off, in time with the beat.

As they skirted the main dance floor, Jasper caught one sickening sight after another — men and children, boys and girls, at the bar and in booths, making out. One man, a guy who had to be at least sixty, was getting blown by a girl who couldn't have been more than eight.

He wanted to put a bullet in the fucker's head right there, grab the girl, and free her.

It was all Jasper could do to turn away from the horrors before him. And this was right out in the open. God only knew what disgusting acts were happening in the rooms. This wasn't paradise, it was something out of Dante's Inferno. Maybe worse.

A pair of women approached them near the exit, flirting, saying something in Spanish. Jasper couldn't hear the guard's response, but one of the women put a gun in Jasper's face and started shouting.

Her pistol went off, but he was already spinning away. He fired three shots into her falling body with the Glock.

Then pandemonium as three things happened at once.

One — the man Jasper had been following took off, disappearing into the crowd.

Two — men, women, and children ran hither and yon in every direction.

Three — automatic gunfire erupted from somewhere in the chaos.

A glass partition shattered behind Jasper.

He shoved the pistol in his waistband, dropped the jacket, raised the AR-15, and ran.

More shots fired. People around him, men and women, fell.

The fuckers didn't care who they were hitting.

Jasper wanted to turn and locate the shooter, but doing so would make him an easy target, and if he didn't know where the bullets were coming from, it would also make him dead.

He slipped into a crowd heading toward the double sets of glass doors at the entrance.

The music kept pumping above the screams of the people, making it impossible to get a feeling for where shots were coming from as the floor and walls were chipped away by gunshots. Staccato lights and unrelenting darkness played with his vision, putting Jasper at a serious disadvantage to his enemies who knew this location far better than him.

Jasper slid into a crowd, lowering his gun, trying not to stand out.

Bodies against him, crying, shouting.

He glanced to his right and down at a young girl who sobbed as she tried to press past the wall of people. Mascara ran down her face as she tried to escape.

A fat man shoved her down, trying to pass her. The crowd behind him followed, trampling the girl. Jasper stopped and threw himself against the tide of people. A man in a suit yelled at him, throwing a punch.

Jasper tossed him aside, into another man, then turned around to find the girl on the ground, face down, wailing and covering her head. Bruises and scrapes marred her young flesh.

Jasper used the rifle's sling to throw it over his shoulder

while he grabbed the pistol from his waistband, then he reached down and picked her up.

"Hold tight." He hugged the girl close to his chest as he pushed toward the door in a crouching jog. Someone yelled behind him and fired a shot. It missed.

Jasper spun around, balancing the girl, praying he wasn't going to use her as a shield, then raised his pistol and fired, hitting the man once in the chest, then again in the head.

The second shot dropped him.

Jasper turned and continued with his awkward jog, clutching the girl, heading into the stream of people, shoving his way past the adults, making way for the children.

Most of the people were running right into the massive lobby and out into the daylight.

He considered racing out with them, but the gunmen would be waiting, and flight wouldn't bring him any closer to Madam.

Jasper spotted two women coming out a door. Above it, a sign indicated stairs.

He ran with the girl, eager to get her somewhere safe before resuming his search.

Just inside the stairwell, Jasper finally had a chance to catch his breath.

"What's your name?" he asked the young girl.

"Rosita."

"Rosita. I'm Jasper. You're okay now. I need to put you down. Okay?"

"No." She stared at him with big, helpless eyes. "Dangerous."

He sighed and looked up the stairs. Now that Jasper was standing still, his adrenaline was petering out, and he

was beginning to feel every bruise that had been inflicted on him.

And climbing the stairs would be a bitch if he had to carry a kid.

But with all hell breaking loose, he had no idea how long he had before more guards came upon him, and he needed a safe place for Rosita before he finished his search for Madam Pandora.

Chapter 43 - Paul Dodd

PAUL PACED THE LIVING ROOM, savoring the moments before his guests awoke.

He was in his new home, a gift from Madam Pandora. A single-story house fifteen minutes from Paraíso, a gated parcel on the outskirts of El Sol Constante, in a wooded area owned by Madam Pandora, and thus private for at least a few acres.

The house was nice, with all modern electronics and appliances, even though the furniture itself looked a decade or so behind the times. It had three bedrooms, a large kitchen, and two baths. The highlight was the basement — a soundproof set which had been used for a number of pornographic films, many illegal, Paul inferred from both what Madam had said and what Daniel told him on the ride over.

Paul had declined having Daniel stay with him. He needed privacy to truly reap the benefits of living here. Daniel arranged to stop by daily, to check and see if Paul needed provisions, until he was ready to go into town himself.

Paul glanced at the television, tuned to the basement's closed-circuit cameras.

He smiled at the sight of Mallory and Jessi, each of them cuffed to twin beds side-by-side.

They were still passed out from the drugs, which gave him more time to work up his appetite.

He'd had fun with the little girl at the hotel, but in the end, she lacked Jessi's innocence, even though she was only a few months shy of eleven.

He had a history with Jessi. Same for Mallory. And he couldn't wait to resume their relationship. There was something about the cop that both drove him crazy with rage, and … turned him on.

He wasn't attracted to many women.

But Mallory was different.

Was it because he'd never fucked a mother and daughter? Perhaps there was some of that. But there was something else, too. A connection to Ashley. The more he looked at Mallory, the more Paul flashed back to his time with her daughter.

No, she hadn't been his favorite at the time, but he'd thought about her often after she was gone. He'd watched videos of her, and of them together, while spilling his seed. There was something about her that never ever bored him.

Most girls, he tired of seeing after a while. Their special thing faded after repeated viewings. This was true of both pornography and recordings of those girls he'd been with in real life.

But Jessi and Mallory stirred something within him. He was aroused just looking at the monitor, imagining what was going to happen. Picturing the both of them under his thumb, begging for their lives as he humiliated them, as he fucked their brains out, over and over and over.

Paul started touching himself as he moved closer to the monitor.

"Wake up, you little cunts. Daddy's waiting."

Chapter 44 - Jasper Parish

JASPER WAS CARRYING Rosita against his chest as he went door to door knocking, "Security. Open up."

He held the pistol at the ready, but either the rooms were all empty or people were looking out their peepholes and deciding not to open up.

He knocked on a fifth door, this time covering the hole with the back of his hand. "Security, open up!"

"What is it?" asked a man with a British accent.

"We've got a bomb threat. We need to evacuate everybody. It's a level five situation." A bullshit designation might make this more believable.

The door opened to a thin pale man. He looked like a retired accountant or maybe a banker, wearing a silk robe and nothing underneath.

"What's going on?" he asked as Jasper pressed his way inside and closed the door behind him.

A young woman was lying on her stomach, facing the opposite wall. She was either short or underage. Her arms were cuffed to the headboard. Ankles too, legs splayed. Bright red lashes and dark welts covered her legs, back,

and ass. A whip and paddle lay on the edge of the bed, along with lubricants and toys.

Jasper never understood the thrill of bondage, either delivering or receiving pain. Wasn't there enough agony in the world without bringing it into your sex life? It wasn't illegal, so long as these two were consenting adults. But even if the girl on the bed was an adult, he wasn't sure if she could consent — especially if she was a slave.

"Are you okay, ma'am?" Jasper called out.

The man, indignant, shouted, "What the hell is going on here? I'm going to need to see some identification."

The girl turned her head toward Jasper. She was far too young for consent.

"Close your eyes, sweetie," Jasper said to Rosita.

She closed her eyes.

Jasper shot the man in the head.

The girl on the bed screamed. Rosita flinched, but kept her eyes closed.

"I'm not going to hurt you," Jasper promised the girl on the bed.

He set Rosita down on a love seat and after turning it away from the man's dead body, went over to the girl who was twitching and trying to break free of her restraints, practically hyperventilating, eyes wide. She was pulling so hard at the cuffs that Jasper was afraid she might hurt herself.

"I'm not gonna hurt you." Jasper set the rifle and his pistol on the ground and raised his hands.

Rosita said something in Spanish and the girl relaxed.

He found the keys to the cuffs and unlocked them.

She sat up, covering herself with the sheet, staring at Jasper and then at Rosita. The girl looked maybe thirteen.

"Are you okay?" Jasper asked.

Rosita translated.

The girl nodded.

"Okay, you all stay here. I need to go find someone."

"No!" Rosita shouted, getting off the chair and coming over to him. "Don't go. Not safe."

"I'll be okay," Jasper said.

"No. Not safe for us. Please, take us with you."

Jasper stared at the girls and felt utterly helpless. He didn't have time to rescue them or the other people held here against their will. He was only one man, and Madam Pandora had an army.

He would be lucky to find Jessi and Mallory. Stopping to save others might blow his mission to hell — if it wasn't already ruined by that fucker, Anders Martin.

Jordyn was suddenly beside him. "You can't just leave them here."

"What am I supposed to do?" Jasper sighed. "Bring them with me?"

"I dunno."

"Well, neither do I! I need to find them."

Time was running out, the walls were closing in.

Rosita asked, "Who are you looking for?"

"Two of my friends were taken here. A blonde girl, Jessi. And an American woman named Mallory. You haven't seen them, have you?"

Both girls shook their heads.

"I know someone who might be able to help you," Rosita said.

"Who?"

Chapter 45 - Jasper Parish

Jasper and Rosita waited as the older girl, Gloria, went to find Rosita's sister.

If anyone knew where to find Jasper's friends, she would. Rosita's sister helped Madam directly. Jasper wasn't sure he could trust her, but at this point, anyone who could lead him to Pandora was a resource, whether they helped him willingly or by force.

After about fifteen minutes, Jasper was afraid that Gloria had second thoughts and went to tell security about the American who'd come into the room and shot the guest. He imagined squads charging up the stairs in formation, armed to the teeth, throwing gas and storming the place.

He grabbed the AR-15 and told Rosita to back away from the door, to stay in the bathroom.

After what felt like an eternity, there came a knock at the door.

Jasper approached slowly, stepping softly, rifle in hand and ready to fire.

His heart raced as he moved toward the peephole then

saw Maria and another young woman outside.

He opened the door.

The other girl, in her late teens, marched in without any regard for Jasper's gun, or the body on the ground. "Where's my sister?"

Jasper pointed toward the bathroom.

Rosita ran out and jumped into her sister's arms, talking a hundred words a second in Spanish, pointing to Jasper as she spoke. The young woman put Rosita down and offered a hand to Jasper.

"My name is Lucia. My sister said you saved her from being trampled, even though guards were shooting at you?"

Jasper nodded. "She said you'd know where my friends are."

"The blonde girl, Jessi, and the woman?"

Jasper felt a swell of relief, his heart about to burst from his chest. "You *have* seen them?"

"Yes. But they're not here now."

"What?" His elation fell to fear in an instant. Were they dead? To come all this way to have them already be dead, Jasper wasn't sure he could take it.

"That man took them to a house nearby. The bad house."

"What man? What house?"

"Another American. Bald. Scary. I think his name was Paul?"

"Yes, that's him! What about the house?"

"It's where Madam would send girls, and sometimes boys, to make movies with wicked men."

Jasper felt that sickening kick in his gut. This place was a wretched hell for these kids. How long had it been going on and how many had suffered? How many were dead, or worse, still alive and wishing they weren't?

Jasper wanted to ask Lucia why she and Rosita were here. Why didn't they just leave? But now wasn't the time. Besides, he could imagine all too easily how they wound up here. Plenty of terrible avenues led girls to places like this, and they all existed because of two things — the sickness of hideous men and the greed of those who would exploit their children, families, and communities to feed their sick desires. As for why they hadn't left, that reason was always the same. *Fear.*

"Do you know where this place is?"

Lucia nodded.

"Can you bring me there?"

For the first time, terror crept into her face.

Rosita grabbed her sister's arm. "He can help us escape!"

Lucia looked him up and down, looking doubtful. "You look pretty hurt."

"I'm fine," Jasper said.

Lucia turned to Rosita. "Where would we even go? Our family sold our mother to Madam."

"I'll find somewhere for you.," Jasper promised. "For all of you."

Lucia eyed him with suspicion. She looked like someone who had been kicked every time that she'd taken a risk, learning it was better to suffer under a monster you knew than one you didn't.

"*Please,*" Rosita cried, grabbing Lucia's arm. "We can't stay here."

Gloria said something in Spanish, and Lucia nodded. "If I get you to the garage, can you drive?"

Jasper nodded.

"Okay. We'll go. If you promise to help us."

"I swear on my life."

Chapter 46 - Mallory Black

MAL WOKE to the sensation of something pressing hard against her skin.

She opened her eyes, still fuzzy, and saw Dodd fastening a strap on her leg. She was in what appeared to be a wedding dress, upright, limbs outstretched and bound in several places on a giant black platform.

No, not a platform, a wheel. A big wooden spinning wheel.

What the hell is this?

"Ah, you're awake. *Shhh* … you don't want to wake poor Jessi."

Mal looked around and finally found her, lying on a bed, wearing a similar dress.

"You like the outfits? That's the problem with today's culture. Call me old fashioned, but I prefer clothes that leave something to the imagination. That *make* you imagine."

"You sick fuck." Mal spit at him.

He stepped back, wiping the spit from his face, then licked it.

"I'd be careful if I were you, Mallory. Your behavior can go a long way into determining the tone of these next few days."

Mal glared at Paul as he resumed tightening the strap at her ankle.

"Ah, I think that should just about to do it."

He reached behind the wheel and clicked something. "You might want to hold on to those bars." Then he tapped one of the two metal handles near her hands.

She gripped them.

He spun her around, slowly, her stomach going into free fall, her head already swimming.

"Please. I get motion sick easily. I don't want to puke."

He stopped her, upside down, then looked down at Mal, smiling.

"Ah, I like this wheel a lot. I wonder why I never thought to get one for my old place. You know who would've loved this ... Ashley."

"Don't you say her name," Mal growled.

"What's that?" Paul smiled like a deranged lunatic, still looking down at her. She'd never seen him this manic, or so downright scary. He was enjoying every moment, and God only knew what he had in store for them.

Mal flashed back to that night when he had taken her and Jessi to her house, then brought them to Ashley's room, planning to rape Jessi right in front of her. She glanced over at the girl and thought, *Please, God, don't wake up.*

"Put me back right. I'm really going to puke."

"Fine," Paul said, spinning her fast, then stopping the wheel with a sudden grip that forced her stomach into another somersault.

It spasmed, along with her throat, but she didn't throw up.

Paul got in her face, still smiling. "God, I've missed you."

"What do you want from me?"

"Well, I *wanted* to be friends. That's what I wanted. For you to visit me in jail and keep me company. But *noooo*, you had to be a cunt about it."

"You raped and killed my daughter! What did you expect, for us to be buddies? Tell me you really aren't that deluded, Paul."

Using his name softened his crazed glare, just a bit. She made a mental note. It could come in handy. Everybody had a lever. If Mal played this smart, she might be able to get him to free her. But she would have to resist the urge to spit on him or curse him out again.

"You don't get it, do you? I wanted to share Ashley's final moments with you. I thought you'd want to know how her last days went."

"I know how they went."

"No, no you don't. Not really."

He seemed almost earnest.

She played along. "Okay, tell me."

"No. I don't think I want to now."

Mal sighed. Was he really going to play this game? It was all she could do not to call him a whiney moody bitch to his face. "Please. Tell me."

"No. You lost that chance when you sent that message."

"What message?"

"That Nazi fuck who raped me in the shower and nearly killed me. That message!"

"You think I had someone rape you?"

"You threatened me, Mal. Of course I think you did that. You wanted me to feel what Ashley felt. But here's the thing, I wasn't nearly as vicious as that fucking Nazi was! I

was gentle, caring. And when your daughter died, I made it quick and painless."

Mal tried not to let his words slice into her. "I didn't send anyone to hurt you, Paul. As much as I hate you, I would never have someone brutalize you the way you did my daughter. *Never*."

Paul shook his head. "I told you, I was kind and gentle. I know you're going to find this hard to believe, but your little princess liked what I did to her."

"Bullshit!"

Paul reached under her dress, his fingers crawling up her inner thighs.

She squirmed, but there was no point in trying to escape. The bondage wheel was secure.

"Know what she liked most? When I did this."

He began rubbing Mal's clitoris outside of her underwear. She wanted to puke again. She closed her eyes, not wanting to see his smile, knowing it would only make it easier to imagine him doing this to her baby girl.

"Oh, yeah, she liked that a lot. And she liked this even more."

He slipped a finger inside her.

Mal squeezed her eyes tight, flashing back to that moment after Jasper saved her, when he handed her the gun, offering her a chance to kill the monster right there.

Now, as he slipped his finger around inside her, she wished she'd taken that shot.

Mal had tried to do things by the book, to put the murderer in jail where he belonged. But what good was doing things the right way when the jail couldn't even hold him let alone prevent the pedophile from striking again or taking Jessi?

Paul laughed and pulled out his finger. "Of course your daughter wasn't nearly this dry."

She wasn't ready to open her eyes and see that smug fucking face beaming back at her. Not yet. But then, as she heard Paul walking away, she had to see what was happening.

There were two beds on the opposite wall. Beside them, a long table where Paul was heading.

Her eyes were still blurry from whatever she'd been injected with, but she could make out a black bag, the kind that doctors used to carry back when they still made house calls, long before she was born.

"This," Paul said loudly for Mal's benefit, "used to be a movie set. Well, I use the term 'movie' loosely. Mostly for illegal pornos and snuff films. I was pleasantly surprised when I saw all the props they left behind."

He pulled something out of the bag, then started walking toward her, keeping the item hidden behind his back. Mal swallowed, bracing herself for whatever the hell he was about to bring over.

And then he showed her — a gun, which he pressed hard against her forehead.

He laughed. "Yeah, they left a loaded gun here! Imagine that. I wonder if it works. Let's say we test it!" He turned the pistol toward Jessi's bed.

"No!" Mal screamed. "Don't!"

Paul turned, smiling. "Why shouldn't I? Don't you think it's a bit cruel to let her live through what I'm going to do to you both?"

"Please, Paul. You don't need to hurt us. You can let us go. You can live out your life here in Mexico and no one will look for you."

"Bullshit! I'm a wanted man, Mallory. You really think I believe you won't come looking for me?"

"I swear. Just let her go. She's been through enough."

Paul closed his eyes. "What about me? What about

what I've been through?" he screamed, face turning bright red, spittle hitting Mal in her face.

He was all over the place emotionally. She had no idea what she'd touched on, but Mal made another mental note to working on solving the mystery of his psyche and how to get out of this using the only thing she still had — her words.

Paul stomped back over to the bag, put the gun back inside, and grabbed something else. This time he didn't bother to hide the knife. He glared at her, his eyes full of rage.

"Do you know what that Nazi fuck did to me?"

"No," Mal said, trying to sound sympathetic.

"I'm going to show you."

Paul spun the wheel, stopping it so that Mal was horizontal to him. Then he walked toward her head, his crotch level with her face, and unzipped his pants. But instead of pulling anything out, he slipped the knife through the zipper, pretending it was his cock.

He held the blade, pretending to stroke it as he looked down at Mal, his smile now impossibly wider.

"First he made me open my mouth. Open your mouth, Mallory."

She shook her head.

"Open your fucking hole or I'll cut a new one in you!"

Mal opened her mouth.

"Good, now stick out your tongue."

She did.

He pressed the cold blade against her tongue.

The taste of copper coated her throat as Paul drew blood.

She struggled not to choke, as he slipped the blade in deeper. Choking might press it through her tongue or cheek.

She gagged.

He withdrew the blade, but his smile was gone. Now Paul was staring at her as one might look at an experiment, coldly, unemotionally, as he puts his fingers in her mouth and forced her to show the cut on her tongue.

Paul walked back over to the table, laughing as he went. "So, Mallory, while I was in your house, I noticed quite the collection of pain pills. And I got to thinking about my own mother and her addictions. God, you have no idea how much I hated that cunt."

Mal swallowed the blood, stuck in the horizontal position, wondering what the hell he was going to come back with this time.

"And I was wondering, were you always an addict or did you become one after Ashley died?"

"After," Mal said.

"Hmm, I'm not sure I believe you. But, at any rate, I got to wondering, what else have you done, Mallory? What other drugs?"

"Just pills."

Mal wondered what the hell he was doing, hunched over the table. She smelled something burning.

"Really? Why stop there? I hear that heroin provides a much better high. The kind you live your whole life and can never experience again."

"I'm not a junkie."

He turned around holding a hypodermic in his hand and a length of rubber hose between his teeth. "Now, I never did the good stuff myself, but damn, for someone like you, this has to be the ultimate, right? Why not live a little?"

"What are you doing?"

He spun her right side up, put the needle in his mouth, and slipped the hose around her arm, tightening it.

She shook her head. "No, please. Don't."

He laughed. "Oh, come on. You must be curious."

"No, please, Paul. Don't do this."

He tightened the hose, then met her eyes. "You'll thank me later."

Seconds later, he was bringing the needle to her vein.

"Please, don't!"

Too late.

The needle punctured her flesh, and the drug rushed into her bloodstream.

Chapter 47 - Jasper Parish

ESCAPING Paraíso had been easier than Jasper thought it might be, and for once, he felt like the odds wouldn't be impossible to overcome.

Jordyn occupied the front seat of the stolen BMW while Lucia, Rosita, and Maria sat in the back. Lucia leaned forward between the seats, giving directions as Jasper navigated the bumpy roads.

"How you feeling?" Jordyn asked Jasper.

"I think we might make it," he said, though he hated jinxing himself by thinking positively before they were on site and Dodd was either disabled or dead.

"You still seeing the same vision?" Jasper was referencing the standoff, with him about to kill Paul and Mallory arguing about it.

"It's fuzzy," Jordyn said.

Visions rarely changed, so Jasper didn't know if it being "fuzzy" meant that things had already taken a turn for the worse or if they were authoring a new future. Maybe him stopping to save Rosita had altered the earlier timeline.

But Jasper refused to believe that stopping to save the girl or to extract the others out of Paraíso had altered things for the worse. It saved him the trouble of extracting the home's location from Madam. And it had been the right thing to do.

"Who are you talking to?" Lucia asked.

"They can't see me, Dad. Remember?"

"Just thinking things out loud." He looked at Lucia in the rearview, then at the other two girls, both glancing around as if they'd not been outside in ages, even though the scenery was only comprised of trees and the occasional homes, both small and sprawling.

"When's the last time you girls have been out?"

"We were born in Paraíso," Lucia said, then after a pause she added, "But I have been to the bad home twice."

"Jesus."

"Okay, it's coming up on this road. Not too far down." Lucia pointed down a small dirt road, surrounded by thick woodlands on either side.

Jasper turned onto the dirt road and started driving, but much slower. After a few minutes, Lucia pointed to a gate about a hundred yards away. It was open, with an SUV parked inside it.

"The house is just past that gate."

Jasper stopped. "Okay, I'm going in alone. I don't suppose any of you have ever driven a car?"

All three shook their heads.

"Okay, Lucia, come up here and if you see anyone, honk, okay?"

"Okay," she said as she got out of the car and took the front seat.

Jasper pulled out his pistol. "Ever fire a gun?"

Again, she shook her head.

233

Jasper showed her the CliffsNotes while the other girls watched with awe-struck expressions. This was likely the first time anyone had ever given any of them the power to fight.

"Hopefully you won't need to use it, but if you do, don't be scared or think twice. Just aim at their stomach and fire. You got it?"

Lucia nodded.

"Okay." Jasper grabbed the AR-15 from the back seat. "I'll be back in a few minutes. If you see anybody other than me or Jessi or Mallory leave that house, run without looking back. You got it?"

Lucia nodded again. While she'd lived most of her life in fear, this girl was ready to be free, and to fight for that freedom if need be.

Jasper took one last look at all three girls then headed toward the house.

He kept to woods while approaching, hugging the edges until he reached the gate, his eyes on an ever-vigilant lookout. Seeing nobody, he made a break for the gate, crouching on one side of the SUV as he took another look at the small yard in front of the house, and then the house itself.

The windows were all closed, curtains drawn.

He approached the front door with Jordyn behind him but stopped short of trying the knob.

Jasper wasn't about to fall for a trap.

He motioned to Jordyn that they circle back around. They crept around the side, ducking low in front of an open window. They stopped. The faint sound of a television was broadcasting soccer. Beyond that, silence.

He crept carefully around to the rear, and taking a chance, he peered inside one of the open windows.

The TV was blasting, but the room was empty.

According to Lucia, the house had a basement, home to most of the atrocities and probably where Paul was holding his victims.

Jasper reached a set of French doors. Curtains blocked the windows, so he couldn't see inside. But that also meant nobody could see him.

He tried the doorknob.

It started to turn.

He looked at Jordyn and nodded, readying his rifle as he slowly opened the door.

Jasper stepped inside.

As he breached the doorway, a pistol was pressed against his temple from someone hiding just on the other side of the door.

"Drop it, asshole."

Jasper turned to see Anders Martin smiling down the other end of Jasper's Beretta.

Chapter 48 - Mallory Black

THE RUSH of heroin was instantaneous. Liquid heaven straight into her veins.

Whatever high Mal had felt from the pills was an echo of this Shangri-La inside her now.

Ecstasy, even as she tried to fight against it. Tried to keep her wits about her.

She opened her eyes, forcing herself to see the threat, to see Jessi passed out on the bed.

Stay alert!

Paul smiled. "How does it feel?"

Mal didn't answer, though it was hard to find the seething hate she'd been burning with only moments before. Everything was different. She was filled with bliss, and her eyes were so heavy. It would be so easy right now to leave reality.

She closed her eyes again.

Paul leaned in. She could feel him next to her, though it was like he was above the water and she was beneath it.

"You know who else liked the heroin?"

She opened her eyes.

"Jessi."

She looked over at the bed again. Jessi was starting to stir. She had one hand tied to the bed with rope. A second length dangled from the bedpost. He must've untied the girl to inject her.

"You fucker," Mal said, though she wasn't sure if the words came out as sharp as she'd intended. Everything felt so sluggish.

"Mallory?"

Paul turned. "Ah, she's awake! We're finally back from commercials." He went over to a tripod in the corner and turned on a camera, aiming it at Jessi on the bed. "We're gonna make us a little movie down here, ladies. I'm gonna call it, *Picking Up Where We Left Off.* I know, it's not the best title, but who cares? It's not like people will be seeing it."

Mal was hearing him but not connecting the meaning behind his words.

Picking Up Where We Left Off?

Paul came over to her. "So, let's see, when last we left our ragtag group, they were at Mallory's house, in her daughter's room. And the evil child molester was about to show the detective what he had done to her daughter, so she could feel what she felt in her last days. So, action!"

Paul went over to Jessi and lifted her dress.

She tried to push him off of her but was doing a terrible job, drugged as she was and tied to the bed.

"Stop it!"

Paul hopped off the bed, ran over to Mallory, and got in her face. "You want me to stop? Then how about you and me play a little game?"

"What?"

"How about you be Ashley, and I'll be your daddy." He reached under her dress again and roughly grabbed her.

"Fuck you," she said, before remembering what that had earned her the last time.

He reached behind the wheel and unlocked something. Then it spun, fast.

Mal's world became a stomach churning blur.

Paul started walking away.

She desperately tried to follow his movements, battling the urge to throw up and make sense of the blur. He was at the table when the wheel finally slowed.

He picked up the knife and brought it over to Jessi's bed. "Spread your legs, little girl."

Jessi cried out, and Paul slapped her hard.

Mal was upside down as she saw him split her legs with his knees, roughly holding her down.

"What's it gonna be, Mallory? You gonna play Ashley or am I going to fuck Jessi in the cunt with this knife?"

Mal screamed, "Okay! I'll be her!"

Paul leaped off the bed and ran over with the knife as Mal kept spinning.

He grabbed the back of the wheel, jerked it until she was right side up.

And then she could hold it no longer.

She puked, getting it all over Paul.

"You cunt!" He slapped her across the face with the back of his hand. "God damn it!" Paul glared at her, "You ruined the dress!"

"Sorry," Mal said, partially meaning it, because the drugs were fucking with her emotions, making her incredibly sad to have ruined the dress.

Hold onto the anger. *Stay alert!*

Paul brought the knife to her chest.

She finally felt a rush of danger.

No, no, no!

For sure it was over. This was it. Paul was going to gut

her, watch her die, then murder Jessi in some horrifying way.

She'd failed.

Just as she'd failed Ashley.

Mallory cried.

Paul stopped, staring at her.

"What? Did you think I was going to kill you, my sweet little angel?" He laughed. "No, no, no. Not yet. We've still got things to do, Ashley. You have a birthday celebration." He stroked her hair, and then her face.

He cut at her dress, but when the knife got stuck he tossed it aside and began ripping the fabric away. It hadn't come completely off, still tangled in the straps of the wheel, but her nakedness was exposed, and Paul was staring at her, up and down, as if entranced.

He turned away, stripping off his own clothes, "I'll be right back after I wash off."

He opened the bathroom door, and while she couldn't see him as he shut the door most of the way, she could hear him turn on the water for a shower.

This was their chance!

She looked at Jessi, crying on the bed, and whispered, "Psst!" a few times until Jessi finally looked up. "Can you get free?"

Jessi reached up and clawed at the rope's big knot, but then after a minute of frustrating failures she cried out, "I can't."

"Keep trying. You can do it."

Her eyes were glassy, and she could barely focus. The poor girl was probably sleepy as hell from the heroin, her every movement a struggle.

She could hardly focus herself, but after she thought Paul was going to stab her, Mal's adrenaline shook off

some of the drug's effects, forcing her into alertness. They would both die if she didn't.

There would be no rescue this time. It was all up to them.

Jessi was still struggling with the knot when the shower went silent.

"Psst!"

Jessi looked up.

Mal shook her head then nodded at the bathroom.

Jessi looked over, then immediately laid her head back down and closed her eyes.

Good girl.

Paul sauntered out of the bathroom, a white robe clinging to his wet body. He couldn't be bothered to fully dry off. He was carrying a wet towel. He glanced at Jessi, then went to the table, grabbed the pistol, and came over to Mal.

"I'm going to unfasten your straps and we're going to go over to the bed. You do anything stupid, I'll kill you both. But not before I hurt Jessi and make you watch. Understood?"

"Yes."

"Yes, what?"

Mal was confused, then remembered the game.

"Yes, Daddy," she said, swallowing her vomit.

Chapter 49 - Jasper Parish

"I said drop it," Anders repeated.

"Come on, man. You're really going to let him kill a child and a cop?" Jasper still gripped the AR-15, knowing he was flirting with death.

"Drop it."

Jasper lowered the gun, then carefully set it on the floor.

"I knew you'd come here," Anders said, before ordering Jasper down onto his knees.

"Come on, man. You're better than this."

Anders laughed. "Says the man who kidnapped my wife and child?"

"I wasn't going to have them hurt."

"Yeah, whatever. Put your hands behind your head."

"What are you going to do?"

"I'm taking you back to Madam Pandora. She has some questions for you."

"I'll go. But, please, don't let him butcher them. Jessi's just a kid. Come on, Anders. You've got a daughter. You can't—"

"Shut up! Get your hands behind your fucking head."

He was getting to the man. Jasper had a flash of Anders losing it. Snapping and taking a swing. He just had nudge him a little closer to the edge, but not so far that Anders emptied the gun into Jasper's head.

"How'd you feel if it was your little girl down there? Getting raped by that—"

And that did it. No father wants to imagine his child being raped. The image was too much. Anders swung with the butt of the gun. Jasper anticipated, dodging just as Anders was about to connect with his skull.

He reached out, grabbed the gun, then wrenched it upward, crushing Anders's fingers in the trigger guard and forcing him to release it.

Jasper went to fire, but Anders moved too quickly, somehow knocking the pistol from his hand and sliding to Jasper's left.

When Jasper dove for the weapon, Anders rushed him, kicking the gun into the kitchen as Jasper fell to the ground.

Anders kept running, putting himself between the fallen gun and Jasper.

He had a blade in his left hand, his right fingers likely still in pain from being crushed with the trigger guard.

Their gazes locked.

Anders swung and missed.

Jasper backed away, scanning his surroundings. To his left, an island with a rack of pans hanging just over his head. He reached for the closest one.

Anders thrust the blade toward his gut.

Jasper fell backward, just missing the pan, his adrenaline pumping so hard that he didn't know if he'd been stabbed.

No time to look. Anders was coming again.

Jasper dodged, leaning on the island and leveraging himself to the left, quickly maneuvering to the opposite side, reaching up as he went and grabbing a heavy frying pan.

Their gazes locked again.

Jasper was right on top of the gun but had no time to bend over and grab it.

He kicked it back instead, now a loss for them both.

It was a frying pan versus a knife.

Jasper took a defensive stance, waiting for Anders to take another jab. "Last chance to walk away."

"Fuck you." Anders moved in.

Jasper swung, hitting the back of his hand, hard. Somehow the fucker managed to hang onto the blade. He moved in for another jab.

Jasper dodged it, narrowly, then smashed the pan into Anders's jaw.

He fell backwards onto the floor.

Jasper threw the pan at his face, then dove for the gun.

Anders raised his arms to blunt the impact. Then he leapt up, coming at Jasper again with the blade.

His hand closed around the pistol's grip as Anders moved in fast.

Nine times out of ten, given the choice between a knife and a gun in close quarters, the blade won hands down. Speed was almost always on the cutter's side. But this was the tenth.

Jasper raised the pistol and fired four shots in rapid succession.

Anders kept coming, and his blade sunk into Jasper's gut as he fell on top of him.

Anders, though hit, was still trying to end Jasper's life.

He twisted the knife.

The gun was trapped between them, Anders's weight

pressing down on him as he kept twisting the blade into Jasper's stomach.

Pain and adrenaline battled as Jasper struggled to bring the barrel of the gun up just enough to—

He emptied the clip into Anders. The man finally stopped moving.

Jasper shoved the dying asshole off of him then looked down at the front of his body, covered in blood, the knife sticking out of his gut.

"Fuck."

Chapter 50 - Mallory Black

DODD KEPT his gun as he ordered Mal to lie on the bed and slip one cuff around the bed post and another around her wrist.

He'd cleaned her off and given her another dress to wear. This one was pink with what looked like bloodstains peppered across it. Mal suggested that she didn't need it. He corrected her.

"No, I like the slow reveal."

Ah, a rapist who doesn't like to rush into things. How nice.

Still, it might afford Jessi more time to free herself from the knot. And if she could do that, maybe she could get the knife or the gun. They were both lying on the table behind her. Mal would elongate this rape if it meant giving Jessi a chance to save them.

She locked the cuff onto her wrist.

Paul checked it, tugging at it and the one attached to the bed post.

"Good." He smiled, then glanced over at Jessi before turning back to Mal.

"Now, let us begin, *Ashley.*" He stood over the bed, looking down at Mal, licking his lips. "Whose been a naughty birthday girl?"

Fuck, I don't wanna play this game.

Everything about this man repulsed her. His pervert's glare and missing teeth, the erection he kept fondling through the silk robe as he eyed her up and down.

"I've been a naughty girl," Mal said.

"Been a naughty girl, what?"

"Daddy."

He smiled.

She wondered if this was all some fantasy acting out what he wanted to do to his own daughter. According to his ex-wife, he'd never touched Lily, though he *had* taken photos. Maybe he'd been waiting for her to turn ten, too.

He reached down, squeezing her breast through the dress. "Ah, look who's growing up. Such a sweet little girl. Have you been wanting Daddy to touch you?"

Mal nodded. "Yes, Daddy. Please, touch me."

He traced his hand down her stomach, and as he did, she took a chance to look behind him, where Jessi was opening her eyes.

Good girl. Now untie the rope.

Mal's heart began to race at the prospect of Jessi getting free, but there was a fear swelling inside her of what Dodd might do if he caught her. He'd threatened to rape her with a knife.

Would he really do it?

She had to keep him distracted. And play his sick game.

"Touch me there, Daddy," she said, taking her free hand and putting it on his to guide it down.

He rubbed Mal through her dress. She closed her eyes and moaned, "Oh, Daddy."

"Oh, Ashley," he said.

She could take him looking at her like a piece of meat. She could take him touching her most private of areas. She could endure almost anything, but when her daughter's name came out of his fucking mouth, she wanted to sink the claw end of a hammer into his skull.

She reached down, stroking his cock.

It was hard, and touching it sent shivers of revulsion through her.

She imagined him forcing himself inside her daughter and wanted to vomit again.

Play along. Not much longer. Just do this until Jessi can get free.

But would Jessi be able to shoot Paul?

The pistol was a Smith & Wesson .45 with an external safety. Mal wasn't sure if the safety was on or off. And the chances that the girl knew how to fire the gun were probably nil. Even if the safety was off, would she have what it took to pull the trigger? And even if so, would she be able to hit him?

If Jessi didn't fire, or worse, fired and missed, what would he do to her?

The more Mal thought about it, the worse the scenarios that played out in her head.

She might have to disable Dodd herself. But she was dizzy, and the world was still in slow motion. She wasn't sure if this was the normal effects of heroin — he'd given her a lot — or if it was laced with something else. But she was afraid to make a move that would get them both killed.

She'd give Jessi a chance. And if she froze or failed, Mal would figure something out.

Mal looked up at Dodd as he lifted her dress. As the bottom went over her chest, it gave her some cover to take a look over at Jessi. She was clawing at the rope and seemed to be making progress.

But the more she made, the more Mal was afraid that she'd make a noise and attract Dodd's attention.

"Lick me, *Daddy*," Mal moaned, spreading her legs.

"Okay, Ashley," he said, going down on her, pulling her underwear aside.

She couldn't see his face, nor feel him against her. But if she could get him to go down on her, she might be able to get him in a leg lock and buy Jessi time.

She glanced over and saw her slip free of the rope.

Yes!

Mal's heart raced as Dodd licked her legs, biting them softly, then harder.

"Ow!" Mal cried out without meaning to. The last thing she wanted was for Dodd to stop and sit up, and maybe notice Jessi freeing herself. "More, Daddy."

He bit her again.

Hard.

She gritted her teeth, enduring the pain.

She wondered if Dodd was drawing blood.

Jessi slipped off the bed, slowly.

She made her way to the table.

And grabbed the gun.

Mal locked her legs around his head. "Now!"

Dodd screamed, trying to push her off of him.

"Shoot him!" Mal yelled.

He punched her hard, repeatedly, in the ribs.

She tried to fend him off, twisting, writhing to keep his head inside her leg lock.

Then he bit her leg so hard that she had to let go.

Mallory screamed.

Dodd leaped up, then turned and froze at the sight of Jessi aiming the gun.

"Get away from her!" Jessi shouted, the gun shaking in her hands.

Mal didn't instruct her to shoot him, afraid that she wouldn't be able to. Better to use the fear that she might shoot him. That was the only way to make this man obey or stand down.

"Back up," Mal ordered.

He turned to her, laughing. "She's not going to shoot me."

"Yes, I will!" Jessi shouted, fire in her eyes. "You killed my Daddy!"

The gun was shaking wildly. Though it wasn't particularly big, it looked giant in her hands, and her arms looked spindly trying to steady it.

So much could go wrong.

Mal had to take control of the situation. "Get on your knees, Dodd!"

"Fuck you," he said starting toward Jessi.

Jessi pulled the trigger.

Nothing.

"It's a fucking prop!" Dodd stormed towards her.

Jessi dropped the gun and grabbed the knife from the table.

Mal struggled to free her wrist from the cuffs — she didn't even care if she tore her hand clean off — to get between them.

Dodd kept coming.

Jessi grabbed the blade.

She went to jab at the monster. But he stepped aside and shoved her. Hard.

Jessi fell backward at an unnatural angle, her head cracking the table as she collapsed to the ground.

He stared at her.

She wasn't moving.

Blood pooled beneath her head, turning her blonde hair red and sticky.

Mal screamed, her heart shattered.

Dodd held the blade, then looked down at Jessi's body. "Why the fuck did you have to do that? I wasn't gonna fucking kill you!"

He cursed more, hitting himself in the head several times as he screamed "damn it" repeatedly.

His plans had just gone to shit.

Dodd turned, looking at her with pure hate. "This is *your* fault."

Then he came at her, blade in hand, ready to end Mallory's life.

Chapter 51 - Jasper Parish

JASPER LEFT the knife in his gut. He didn't dare remove it and risk leaking to death.

He was looking for the basement, staggering, when he heard the woman's scream.

Only when he reached the door did he check his ammo. One bullet in the chamber, then he was empty. He hadn't thought to search Anders for another magazine.

He thought of going back, but there wasn't time. He looked at Jordyn, coming up behind him. "Should I get bullets?"

"There's no time. He's going to kill her."

Jasper burst through the door, hoping like hell he could get Dodd to stand down with just the threat of shooting. He was in no shape to fight.

Dodd was on top of Mallory, holding a knife to her throat.

"Stand down!" The yelling took effort, and he was losing blood fast, dizzy and weak.

Dodd turned. "You again? What the fuck is your deal, man?"

Jasper steadied his aim. "Get off of her."

"Shoot him!" Mal shouted.

When he *wanted* to shoot the bastard, Mallory fought him. Now that he only had one shot and might very well miss, she wanted him to take it.

Jasper yelled, "Get off of her!"

Dodd stayed put, blade to her throat, straddling Mallory.

As Jasper stepped into the room, he saw Jessi bleeding to death or already dead on the ground.

He wanted to put a bullet in the bastard right now. But if he missed or the shot didn't incapacitate him, then he might slit Mallory's throat as one last act of defiance before leaving this world.

"Get off of her now, or I will kill you."

"I'm not going back. And … you don't look too good, buddy."

"You're either going back or you're going under. Your choice. I don't care."

"You may as well kill me," Dodd said, staring at Mallory.

Jasper continued toward them, the gun shaking in his hand.

And then he fell.

Chapter 52 - Mallory Black

MAL SHRIEKED as Jasper fell to the ground.

No!

Dodd hopped off of her, still holding the knife, and went over to Jasper, now lying motionless with his face on the ground.

Mal hoped he was faking. Maybe when Dodd went for the gun, Jasper would flip over and blast him, ending the monster once and for all.

Dodd picked up the gun, laughing as he turned to Mal. "Well, looks like the cavalry ain't coming to save you this time."

Jessi was dead.

Now Jasper was gone, too.

And Mal was beyond caring if she died. A part of her just wanted the pain of living to end right now.

"Do it," she said.

"What?"

"Kill me like you did my girl. Then, at least, I can be with her."

Dodd stared at Mal, then shook his head. "I asked you

to kill me last time, but noooo, you had to arrest me. *You should have fucking killed me!* Then none of this would've happened. I wouldn't have been raped, and they wouldn't be dead. But you couldn't do it. You had to be the hero."

"Fuck you."

"No, Mallory. Fuck you. And now I'm going to make you regret your entire pitiful life. I'll kill you, but only after you're begging for death. Only after you feel what Ashley felt."

Dodd started toward her.

"Fuck you! No wonder your wife left. She saw you for the coward you are! A worthless chicken shit pervert who wanted to fuck his own daughter."

"You shut your mouth," he said, aiming the gun at her.

"Is that it, that why you want me to call you Daddy? You thinking of your precious Lily?"

"Don't you mention her name!"

"Ah, that's it, isn't it?" Mal laughed, long and cruel. "Why didn't you rape your own daughter instead of taking mine? Was she too slutty for you? Is that it?"

He fired a shot.

Mal closed her eyes, waiting for the end.

And then the gun clicked.

She opened her eyes.

Dodd was out of bullets. All he had was his knife.

But Mal had her feet and one arm.

"Come on, fucker," she dared him, squatting on the bed and waiting for him to make a move.

She would either die and finally join Ashley or find a way to escape.

He started toward her, eyes full of hate.

"You fucking c—"

A thunderous explosion.

Chips flew from the drywall to Mal's left.

A high-pitched scream flooded Mal's ears as she looked for the source of the gunshot.

Lucia, standing in the door, aiming a gun at Dodd.

He turned around. She fired again and hit him in the knee.

Dodd fell. Lucia stepped into the room, her gun still on him.

Mal yelled, "Get the keys. They're on the table."

Lucia stepped around Dodd, past Jasper and Jessi, staring at them with tears welling in her eyes.

She found the keys and threw them to Mal.

Mal opened the cuff, freed herself, and went to Lucia. "Thank you."

Lucia handed her the gun.

She turned it on Dodd, lying on the ground and writhing in pain.

Mal was about to pull the trigger when she heard a gasping behind her. She turned to see Jessi moving, her eyes blinking.

"Mal?" she said, her voice weak.

"Jessi!" Mal turned and went to her, looking at Jessi's head to see the damage.

There was a big knot, and blood, but it wasn't nearly as bad as she'd thought. Her eyes could barely focus, and her speech was slurred as she looked up and saw Jasper.

"He's … he's dead?"

Mal went to his body and turned him over. Jasper groaned. He shouldn't be alive. He'd lost a lot of blood, and the knife had come loose from his stomach. "Jasper?"

He groaned again, opening his eyes, seeing Mal and then looking at Dodd. "Kill him."

"Hang on," she said. "I'm going to get help for you and Jessi."

"Jessi? She's … she's alive?" He struggled to turn and

managed to smile when he saw her. Then gurgled blood through the wound in his abdomen.

Mal called out to Lucia, "See if there's any first aid kits in the house. And a phone, if there is one."

Lucia nodded then ran from the room. "I need you both to hang on. We're going to get you help."

Mal stood and walked toward Dodd, looking down at him, remembering every horrible thing he'd done to her, to Jessi, to Ashley, and imagining what he'd done to other girls, a number she didn't know, or ever want to discover.

"Please," he cried. "You don't have to arrest me."

"Oh, I'm not arresting you." She aimed the pistol at his head.

"No, no, no! You don't have to kill me, either. I have something, something you'll want."

Mal shook her head, "I doubt that."

"I have a list. A list of the members of Voluptatem. And evidence on them. There are a lot of powerful people on there. Americans. People you may know."

"Where is it?"

"I gave the flash drive to Madam Pandora."

"Too bad," Mal said, focusing her aim.

"Wait! I put a copy online. It's encrypted, but I can get it for you. You can save so many people, Mallory."

"Listen to him," Jasper said.

Mal turned, hardly able to believe that he was asking her to show the monster any mercy. "What?"

"I want that list. We can save others like Lucia, like Jessi."

Mal turned back to Dodd, eagerly nodding. "You can save so many people."

His every word reminded her of the vile things he'd said only moments before. How he would rape Jessi with a

knife. How he'd made Mal pretend to be Ashley to make her feel what she'd felt.

"Why? Why did you do all this? Why did you hurt my little girl?"

"I don't know," Dodd said, tears streaming down his face. "I'm … I'm broken."

"Broken, but you're not really sorry."

Dodd wiped at his tears, "I am. I swear. If I could take it all back, I would."

"But you can't."

Jasper, behind her, said, "Don't do it, Mallory."

"You wanted me to feel what my daughter felt, right?" She placed the gun against his head. "I asked you a question."

"Please …" he cried.

"Don't do it, Mallory!"

She could hear Jasper moving, trying to crawl toward her.

"Answer the fucking question, Paul. Did you want me to feel what Ashley felt?"

Tears were streaming down her face.

Dodd nodded.

"Then I want the same for you."

She pulled the trigger, then fell to her knees.

Lucia came back into the room, staring at Mal, holding a first aid kit and a phone.

Tuesday

Epilogue 1

TWO DAYS LATER ...

JASPER WOKE to a woman's voice. "Is he okay?"

He looked up.

It was Lucia, talking to a doctor.

The man spoke in Spanish, and Jasper could catch only fragments.

He slowly realized that he wasn't in a hospital or a doctor's office. He was surrounded by pictures of dogs and cats. Spanish charts instructing people on how to care for their pets, recognize various symptoms.

Lucia came over. "You're alive."

"Where are Jessi and Mallory?"

"Mallory left this morning. She took Jessi back to the States."

"Are they okay?"

"Yes. Dr. Martinez patched you up and made sure Jessi was okay before they left."

Jasper looked up at the man, confused. "How … how did you find him?"

"He sometimes comes to Paraíso to work on girls when we can't get a doctor to come, or if we need to keep things quiet."

Jasper sat up, too quickly. A sharp pain pierced his stomach.

Dr. Martinez said something in Spanish.

Lucia translated. "He said to be careful, your stitches might pop out."

"We can't stay here. He'll tell Madam Pandora."

"No," Lucia said. "He's not a bad guy."

The man was in his sixties, with wild white hair and the slumped shoulders of a man who had suffered a lifetime of too much shit. Jasper wasn't sure if he could trust him, but if Lucia did, he'd have to as well.

"Where are Rosita and Maria?"

"Maria's in the car with Tony."

"Who's Tony?" There were too many new people for Jasper to process, too many loose ends which might fray and endanger them all.

"Her cousin. He lives in town."

"Can you trust him?"

"Yes. He's letting us stay there."

"What are you going to do? You can't stay here, right? Madam will have people looking for you, for us?"

"Paraíso got raided by the police last night. Not sure who got arrested, but there were lots of people talking about it on the news. Madam Pandora wasn't there."

"Good. I'm glad they shut the place down."

"Tony's got a friend who can get us work in Juarez. He also knows someone who can get you back over the border, once you're ready."

"Thank you." Jasper squeezed her hand.

"You asked about Rosita." Lucia smiled. "She wanted to say something to you."

Lucia left the room, then returned moments later with Rosita, who approached Jasper's bedside, smiling and looking at him with her big brown eyes. She looked so different dressed like a kid in red shorts and a blue tee.

"Thank you, Mister." She hugged him. He flinched as her elbow brushed against his bandage. "Sorry."

"It's okay." Jasper hugged her back. "Thank *you.*"

Epilogue 2

MAL LAY in her hospital bed watching the news conference with Sheriff Bell announcing that Jessi Price and Deputy Mallory Black had both been returned home safely. She'd been admitted for exhaustion and blood work to make sure she hadn't contracted any diseases from the needle in Mexico, or anything else that might have happened while she was out cold. Mal was more exhausted from all the people she had to talk to and reports to fill out since she came back than she was from her ordeal.

Reports where she omitted important details, such as Jasper's name, Lucia's involvement, and how exactly Paul Dodd had come to die. Mal said it was self-defense.

She hoped like hell the Mexican authorities didn't contradict her account. Judging from the Mexican officers she'd spoken to, things looked good for her. They had their own scandal to worry about, including higher-ups that had looked the other way for so long while Madam Pandora ran her illegal brothel and murder compound.

Someone knocked on her door. "Come in."

It was Mike and his wife, Gina, with flowers and a giant *Get Well* mylar balloon.

"How are you?" Gina asked.

"Still alive. Sorry, Mike. You're not getting rid of me that easily."

"Damn it." He reached into his jacket pocket, pulled out a gift-wrapped square, and handed it to her.

"What's this?"

"Well, detective, maybe you should try opening it."

"Fuck you, Mike."

Gina laughed.

Mal peeled the wrapping paper away to reveal a CD. She turned it over, saw it was *ABBA's Greatest Hits*, and laughed. "Thanks, Mike."

"Sorry. I looked for it on 8-track, figuring you probably don't have a CD player yet."

She flipped him off. "So, how's Jessi?"

"Okay. Colleen is glad to have her home."

"That poor kid," Gina said. "And her mother. She's probably never going to let her out of her sight again."

"Paul Dodd won't be coming back this time," Mal said.

A silence crossed the room, and Mal wondered what Mike was thinking. Did he suspect she'd killed him? And if so, how long before he asked her what really happened?

She could lie to a lot of people, even herself. But lying to Mike was next to impossible.

After some more small talk, Gina hugged Mal goodbye, saying she had to use the restroom, though all three of them knew it was to give her and Mike some time alone.

As the door closed, he met her gaze.

Just like that, everything she'd been through, from the kidnapping to Dodd's attempted rape of her and Jessi, to him injecting her with heroin, to her thinking she'd watched Jessi and Jasper die, to her pulling the trigger and

ending the monster's life … all of it toppled down onto her.

And she sobbed.

Mike hugged her tight. "It's okay, you're home now. Everything will be okay."

Mal wasn't sure if everything would ever be okay again. She had leapt over a line she promised never to cross, ending a man's life in cold blood as he begged.

She'd pulled the trigger. And that made her no better than the vigilante, Jasper.

Dodd was gone, and so was all the anger and hate she'd felt for him, for what he did to Ashley. All the rage she had carried so long had disappeared, and now she felt nothing.

That absolute emptiness took root in her soul.

Despite Mike's assurances that everything would be okay, Mal wasn't sure she could ever find her way back to normal.

This was the end of a chapter, and now she had only pain and regret. Once Mike left to go home, she'd be all alone with nobody to understand or help make things better.

Only the taste of heroin had given her hope.

And even as part of her was preparing for her return to work, another was searching for a way to find that sort of bliss again.

Perhaps the only thing to fill the void.

Epilogue 3

THREE DAYS LATER...

JESSI WAS LYING in bed with HappyCorn reading a book her mom had gotten her, a fantasy about a young girl who wakes up in another world. She was hoping it would provide some escape from the horrible memories running through her head but was finding it hard to concentrate.

All she could think about was Officer Mallory shooting the monster in his head.

She told the police in Mexico and here that she didn't remember what happened because she was passed out. But the truth was, she could never forget what she saw.

And, for reasons she couldn't understand, it made her incredibly sad. She should be happy he was gone, and that he suffered for what he'd done to them and to her father. And a part of her was glad. But another part felt bad for Mallory.

She saw something in Miss Mallory's eyes right after

she pulled the trigger — an emptiness that Jessi felt, too. She wished there was some way to make her feel better.

Maybe she'd think of something, but even if she did, Jessi would have to do it on her own. She didn't dare tell her mother what really happened. Mom was honest to a fault, and Jessi didn't want to tell her something that would rip up her insides.

It would be her secret. Her burden to carry. The least she could do for the woman who risked so much to save her. Twice.

A knock on the door.

Jessi didn't feel like seeing her mom right now. She'd left the living room because she'd been too clingy all morning, asking her how she was like every five minutes.

"You have company," Mom said from the other side of the door.

Then she opened it and Destinee was there. Jessi leapt from her bed and raced into a hug.

"Oh, my God, I'm so glad you're okay!" Destinee hugged her back, both of them crying.

"I thought I'd never see you again, either!"

Jessi's mother closed the door and left the girls alone.

"Thank you so much for trying to save me! That was so brave of you."

"Nobody messes with my friend," Destinee said, raising her fists. "Hey, wanna see something cool?"

"Okay."

Destinee lifted her shirt, showing a pink and brown circular gash on her stomach. "My battlescar."

"Oh, my God, I'm so sorry."

"No, it's cool! I mean, yeah, it would've sucked if I died, but I didn't, so it's freaking awesome. Plus, all the kids wanna be my friend now. Even Amber Carrington!"

"No way!"

"Yeah. And … believe it or not, she's not that bad."

"Stop it!" Jessi punched her in the arm.

"She's not as cool as you, but she's not a total b-word, either. And if your mom ever lets you come back to school, I'll make sure she puts you in with the cool kids. Not that you aren't already the coolest kid around. Everyone's asking about you."

"Yeah, not sure I like that."

"Relax, I'll tell them to back off if it's too much."

"Thanks."

They hugged again, and Jessi felt like *maybe* things might finally return to something like normal. Maybe she could be a friend to Mallory like Destinee was to her — someone to make her smile again.

Epilogue 4

Two weeks later ...

Jasper Parish stood in the dark bedroom waiting for the door to open, holding his suppressed pistol.

He listened as the car pulled up outside.

Then he waited for the door to open.

There were two voices, hers and his.

He waited, slowing his breathing and preparing.

The door opened, the lights went on.

Oscar Gonzalez entered, leader of a drug cartel that had scared residents, political figures, and especially reporters who'd found their numbers thinned whenever they wrote a story about him.

He was drunk as he entered, not expecting company.

"Who—"

Jasper fired the pistol twice, hitting him in the head both times.

His body stood for a full twenty seconds before it fell to

the ground, just as Madam Pandora walked in and screamed.

"Quiet or you join him!" Jasper said, gun trained on her.

"Do you realize who you just killed?"

Jasper laughed. "Do I look worried?"

"You should be."

"Listen up. You get one chance to live. I want something you have."

She glared at him. If she was worried about dying, Madam played it cool. "What?"

"The flashdrive."

"I don't have it."

"Then you're no use to me," Jasper said, firing just to the right of her head.

She screamed, finally showing emotion.

"Last chance."

"It's in the safe." She pointed to a spot in back of him. "Behind that painting."

Jasper glanced at the oil of an ocean, then pulled it off the wall. He looked at the safe, then back at Madam. "What's the combination?"

"How do I know you won't kill me after I give it to you?"

"Tell me the combo, then I'll give you a twenty second head start."

She told him.

Then ran.

Jasper opened the safe and found weapons, cash, drugs, and the flashdrive.

He pulled a small flattened black duffel from his pocket and stuffed the contents of the safe into the bag, all except for the weapons. No need for those.

He took the flashdrive last and dropped it in his pocket.

Then he opened the window, looked outside, and saw Madam's car backing out of the driveway.

He raised his pistol and fired six times into the car.

He watched as it kept moving backward, then hit the wall outside the house across the street.

Her body slumped forward and the horn began to blare.

Jasper left. Time to head back home, talk to Spider, see whose names were on the list.

And then he had work to do.

THE END

A quick favor...

If you liked *No Return*, then *would you kindly** consider taking a few minutes to leave a review on your favorite bookselling site. If you're a book blogger, we'd love any mentions on your blog or YouTube channel, also. Every bit of word-of-mouth helps to introduce us to new readers.

As always, thank you for reading,
David Wright (and Nolon King)

(* *Bonus points if you got the* Bioshock *reference.*)

Want More?

Sign up for the FREE newsletter and get a free copy of the King & Wright novel 12.

Join the list and be the FIRST to get the latest news, sneak peeks at what's coming next, and free books and short stories. Our subscribers make our careers possible, and we'll never spam you.

GET YOUR FREE BOOK NOW!

A Note From The Authors

If you're one of those readers that loves to skip to the Authors' Note before you read the story, please turn back now as there WILL be spoilers for *No Return*.

More than any other series so far, Nolan and I knew the trajectory *No Justice* would take from the first book. We had *No Return* in mind as we wrote the series opener, knowing that we wanted to lead up to a big showdown between Paul Dodd and Mallory Black.

We knew that Dodd would be back, which is why we seeded bits into the second and third books, reminding you that hey, this guy is still out there, and a threat.

We knew that he would take Jessi again.

And we knew that we wanted to mirror the first book's ending. We like symmetry here at Collective Inkwell. The ending of *No Return* felt like an awesome season finale if *No Justice* were a TV show.

The only thing we weren't sure about was whether or not Mal would pull the trigger.

We wrestled with this decision for months.

I lost sleep not wanting to fuck things up.

On the one hand, we wanted Mal to remain a hero — to not cross that line. She is a cop, after all. And being a cop, a good cop, is core to her being.

We're in a world that needs heroes, people who stand up to evil, who fight for those who cannot fight for themselves, and, at the end of the day, do the right thing.

On the other hand, Dodd is *really* fucking evil! We've explored with Jasper whether it's ever right to do the wrong thing for the right reasons. It's not an easy question to answer. Doubly hard when it's Mallory having to make the call.

Having gone through what Mal went through, and seeing this vicious child rapist and killer already escape once, who wouldn't want to remove the threat?

Given all that had happened, I couldn't see a way that she *wouldn't* pull the trigger in the heat of the moment. Not this time.

Still, it was one of those moments you can't walk back from. A moment from where there is No Return.

I worried if people would still like Mal. If her choice would disappoint you as a reader. I also wondered if having her kill Paul would erase the line between her and Jasper.

Being worried about these things, I briefly thought about trying to have my cake and eat it too.

(I do like cake. But that's another story.)

So, I thought: *Well, we could make it so she wouldn't have a choice. Where it was either pull the trigger or Paul kills her, Jessi, or Jasper.*

But that would've been cheating.

It robbed Mal of her agency, in having to make that difficult choice.

Also, I hate when fiction takes the easy way out of tough dilemmas.

Still, I wasn't sure I was doing the right thing.

Even up to writing the chapter, I considered having her not pull the trigger. Nolon said he'd back whatever choice I made. Not killing Paul was a way to keep her "good," and would've had our hero sticking to her principles.

However, we already did that ending in the first book. *No Return's* ending wouldn't be nearly as powerful if she made the same choice the second time around.

So, she had to do it.

Had. To.

And, now a couple of months removed from the first draft, I like that Mal pulled the trigger.

I feel bad for her, of course. I love her character, and I know that this action will have some deep ramifications for her. And things are not going to be easy.

However, I'm guessing you read books for the same reason we do — to see people get into shit and try to find their way out. It's kinda what makes thrillers work.

Another concern I had in this book was whether or not Paul was "too evil" this time around.

I liked that he was a realistic villain in the first book. He was conflicted about the things he did. He was a victim who grew into a monster. We could never condone the horrible things he did, of course, but we could *almost* understand what made him what he was.

We always try to get in our villain's heads and see them as they see themselves, to treat them as the hero of their own story. That makes for some very uncomfortable scenes — especially in this book — but I think the best fiction is complicated like that.

Still, we needed to make him even worse this time around, so far gone that you'd be begging for Mal to pull the trigger by the end. Yet, a few times, I thought, *Um, is this going too far?*

It's tough to balance character versus story needs. We tend to err on the side of letting things go too far than playing it too safe. But then we remind ourselves of some of the real-life monsters out there and realize that we probably could've made him even worse.

But, in the end, we go with the characters as they exist in this world.

Characters are what make this series so much fun to write. I love Mal and Jasper because they're flawed and struggling. And no matter how many times they get knocked down by what life is throwing at them, they keep getting up to fight again.

It's not the best example, but I sort of see Creek County as a less political, more thriller version of *The Wire*, a living, breathing world with characters that continue living even after each book is over. A world where small bit characters will play bigger roles down the road, allowing us to tell the sort of stories that work as standalone books, but also reward those who pay attention to the little details. A world I look forward to returning to, to finding out what's going on.

How will Mal bounce back from this moment?

What will Jasper do with the list?

What's going to happen with the upcoming election?

We'll be exploring all this and more when we return to Creek County.

Thank you for joining us on this journey into darkness.

Thank you for reading.

Dave (and Nolon)

About the Authors

Nolon King writes fast-paced psychological thrillers set in the glitzy world of entertainment's power players with a bold, insightful voice. He's not afraid to explore the darker side of human nature through stories featuring families torn apart by secrets and lies.

Nolon loves to write about big questions and moral quandaries. How far would you go to cover up an honest mistake? Would you destroy your career to protect your family? How much of your soul would you sell to get the life of your dreams? Would you cheat on your husband to keep your children safe? Would you give in to a stalker's demands to save your marriage?

David W. Wright is the co-author of edge-of-your seat thrillers including the best-selling post-apocalyptic series *Yesterday's Gone*, the paranoid sci-fi *WhiteSpace* series, and the vigilante series, *No Justice*, as well as standalone thrillers *12*, and *Crash* which was recently optioned for a movie.

David is an accomplished, though intermittent, cartoonist who lives in [LOCATION REDACTED] with his wife and son [NAMES REDACTED.]

He is not at all paranoid.

He is "the grumpy one" on the *The Story Studio Podcast* with fellow Sterling and Stone founders, Sean Platt and Johnny B. Truant.

You can email him at david@sterlingandstone.net

We swear, he almost never bites. Unless you feed him after midnight.

Also By Nolon King

Hidden Justice

Hidden Justice

Hidden Honor

Hidden Shame

Hidden Virtue

No Justice

No Justice

No Escape

No Hope

No Return

No Stopping

No Fear

Once Upon A Crime

Once Upon A Crime

Twice Upon A Lie

Three Times a Murder

Dead For Good

Dead For Good

Left For Dead

Dead Of Night

Wake The Dead

Dead For Life

Stand Alone Novels

Pretty Killer

12

Blown

Miserable Lies

The Target

Secrets We Keep

Close To Home

Heat To Obsession

A Simple Kill

Tell Me No Lies

Red Carpet Black

Fade To Black

Victim

Also By David W. Wright

Hidden Justice

Hidden Justice

Hidden Honor

Hidden Shame

Hidden Virtue

No Justice

No Justice

No Escape

No Hope

No Return

No Stopping

No Fear

Karma Police

Jumper

Karma Police

The Collectors

Deviant

The Fall

Homecoming

Yesterday's Gone

October's Gone

Yesterday's Gone Season One

Yesterday's Gone Season Two

Yesterday's Gone Season Three

Yesterday's Gone Season Four

Yesterday's Gone Season Five

Yesterday's Gone Season Six

Tomorrow's Gone

Tomorrow's Gone Season One

Tomorrow's Gone Season Two

Tomorrow's Gone Season Three

Available Darkness

Darkness Itself

Available Darkness Book One

Available Darkness Book Two

Available Darkness Book Three

WhiteSpace

WhiteSpace Season One

WhiteSpace Season Two

WhiteSpace Season Three

Stand Alone Novels

12

Crash

Emily's List

Threshold